Lost & Bound

A JOSEPHINE STUART MYSTERY

JOYCE OROZ

For information, email Cozy Cat Press,

cozycatpress@gmail.com or visit our website at:

www.cozycatpress.com

ISBN: 978-1-952579-12-7
Printed in the United States of America

10 9 8 7 6 5 4 3 2 1

ACKNOWLEDGMENTS

I AM SO GRATEFUL TO THE VARIOUS PEOPLE WHO INSPIRE, EN-COURAGE AND CORRECT MY WORK. GRACE LAURIN INSPIRED ME, MY READERS HAVE ENCOURAGED ME TO WRITE YET ANOTHER STO-RY AND MY WONDERFUL SUPPORT-GROUP, TOMI EDMISTON, ARTHUR OROZ, FRANK AND MARLENE SHERWIN AND CINDY LAURIN, WHO TOOK TURNS CORRECTING MY MANUSCRIPT.

COZY CAT PRESS PROFESSIONALLY FINE-TUNED EVERYTHING, INCLUDING THE COVER PHOTO TAKEN BY SUPER-PHOTOGRAPHER DAVID NELSON.

MY SINCERE THANKS TO ALL OF YOU.

CONTENTS

Chapter 1 1

Chapter 2 12

Chapter 3 25

Chapter 4 36

Chapter 5 47

Chapter 6 58

Chapter 7 68

Chapter 8 79

Chapter 9 90

Chapter 10 101

Chapter 11 113

Chapter 12 123

Chapter 13 133

Chapter 14 143

Chapter 15 153

Chapter 16 164

Chapter 17 174

Chapter 18 186

Chapter 19 198

Chapter 20 209

Chapter 21 222

Chapter 22 231

Chapter 23 238

Epilogue 248

About the Author 249

Also by Author 250

CHAPTER 1

Halloween night had come and gone along with clear skies, a full moon and peace of mind. Twenty-four hours later everything had changed.

It wasn't the late autumn storm rattling my dining room window that worried me. I can handle rain, wind, fallen trees, mud everywhere, even my patio umbrella flying toward Aromas at low altitude. But I hate it when the electricity goes off! As predicted, the house lights flickered and failed and the TV died.

I groped my way from the living room, through the dining room, to the kitchen. Taking advantage of the occasional flash of lightning, I pushed a chair over to my retro Formica countertop, climbed up and stood on the seat. A sudden clap of thunder had me teetering for a moment. Once I was steady, I opened the upper cupboard door. My fingers explored the top shelf like an octopus groping for guppies. Finally, I felt what I knew was up there, a box of half-burned candles. Thunder roared, a bolt of lightning lit up the kitchen, the box slipped from my fingers and chunky candles pounded the floor.

Seconds later, the house was dark again. Stepping down from the chair one foot found the first roly-poly candle, sending my fifty-year-old derriere up against the refrigerator door. Pulling myself up from the floor with a fat candle in hand, I swiveled toward the counter, felt around and pulled the junk drawer open. Eventually my fingers found a box of matches.

That was the exact moment the lights and Monday night's newscast blinked on. Suddenly the hair on the back of my neck came to attention when the old, trying-to-look-young, TV anchor said, "A woman estimated to be in her early forties was found draped across the top of a large boulder in Felton. According to paramedics, she was unresponsive. Professionals later determined she had died Halloween night." Ms. Anchor reported that authorities were investigating the cause of death and wanted to know the identity of the woman. The deceased woman's picture flashed onto the screen. Instantly she reminded me of someone, but I couldn't name that someone. It was just a feeling that she looked almost familiar.

"You found the body on a rock? In Felton? Are you kidding?" I shouted at the TV, as my voice was drowned out by rolling thunder and thirteen sets of patio wind chimes gone berserk.

My sweet basset, Solow, heard me and crawled out of his hiding place under the coffee table. Putting aside his fear of lightning, he mustered up a speck of courage, probably sensing that he was about to participate in another adventure.

I turned up the TV.

The anchor woman said the Santa Cruz police were investigating.

Suddenly all normal thoughts concerning: my neighbor and fiancé David Galaz, Mom and Dad, my best friend Alicia Quintana, art projects and financial worries were instantly replaced with questions about the probable murder of someone I didn't even know.

In recent years whenever a murder happened, my curiosity drove me to uncover facts pertaining to that incident. Of course, I read murder mysteries and watched them on TV, but whenever a real murder happened on the Central California Coast I invariably felt compelled to search for clues.

Still shaking my head over the odd news, I heard the phone ringing in the kitchen. When I answered with my usual perky hello, Alicia sounded distressed. She seldom became upset over anything, always calm and collected. But over the phone she sputtered and cried her message, something about a terrible thing that happened. Between sobs, she said she'd been watching the seven o'clock news and saw the picture of the mysterious woman. She said she knew the lady who was found lying on top of a large giant rock.

"Allie, hold on, I'm coming over to your house right now. Take it easy." We hung up. I grabbed a jacket, my purse and my comfort dog—Solow. My darling basset, outfitted with short legs and long ears, was all heart and soul. Alicia lived with her husband, Ernie, their ten-year-old son Trigger and a little sheltie dog named Tansy. As it happened, the boys were miles away visiting Ernie's mom in the hospital. Alicia would have gone with them but she had a headache.

As usual, Solow was happy to be going somewhere. I liked to go places too, except when it was stormy. I pulled on my rain jacket and zipped it up over my favorite Sponge Bob jammies. After hoisting Solow into the passenger seat of my old but well-kept red Mazda pickup truck, I rounded the front bumper and climbed into the driver's seat.

Ten miles of treacherous road to Alicia's house in Watsonville felt like a one-hundred-mile journey. I had so many fearful thoughts and questions that I barely noticed how awful the storm was. Leaning into the windshield, I zig-zagged around a large tree branch in my lane and kept going. My little truck thumped into and out of a deep puddle. The headlights glommed onto water crossing the road. I braked, fish-tailed, straightened the truck and kept going.

Alicia had never sounded like she did that night on the phone. Why was she so distraught? I thought of her as the strongest, most down to earth person I'd ever known. She had the perfect husband, a professor of biology at UCSC and a handsome, smart, kind, ten-year-old son. Their house had an up-close view of Drew Lake and her mother-in-law was a gem. All this good stuff began when Alicia was a little six-year-old girl crossing the Mexican border into America with her new adopted parents.

Smart, talented and beautiful, Alicia was a true friend and a valued employee. She and Kyle Larson worked as painters for my "Wildbrush Murals" company. The three of us had painted indoor and outdoor murals all over Santa Cruz and Monterey Counties and beyond.

Kyle, a nineteen-year-old college student with red hair, piercings, a shy smile and an extra-long reach, painted like a dream.

Alicia and I were women of average height and reaching ability.

Skidding to a stop in front of Alicia's two-story house, a glob of southbound leaves smacked the windshield and stuck. I woke Solow and helped him out of his seat. We put our heads down, charged across the squishy front lawn and up a few slippery steps to the front door.

I rang the doorbell.

Seconds later, Alicia opened the door looking dazed. She apologized for bringing us out into the storm.

"Allie, I had to come. I've never heard you sound so upset in all the years I've known you."

Alicia and little Tansy ushered us inside.

"Jo, you're soaked, and look at your slippers."

"I'll just leave them here in the entry." I kicked off the once fluffy slippers and hung up my dripping jacket. We followed Solow into the living room.

"Cover up with that lap blanket, Jo, and I'll make you a cup of hot tea." Alicia hurried into the kitchen. But I didn't care about lap blankets or cups of tea. I wanted to know why my friend was so upset. She'd definitely calmed down since I'd talked to her on the phone, but red puffy eyes and a quiver in her voice gave her away.

Tea and cookies arrived.

My teeth finally stopped chattering when Solow passed out against my feet, warming them up. During daylight hours the Quintana house had the most wonderful view of Drew Lake, a lake big enough for peddle-boats, canoes and row boats but too small for power boats. Fresh rainwater lapped right up to the edge of the back lawn. The living room drapes were still open, allowing a fierce blackness to compete with lamp light and a bright crackly fire in the fireplace.

Alicia sat down on the sofa next to me. "I'm so sorry, Jo. I didn't mean to have you out driving in this weather."

"Allie, just tell me what's wrong."

"I know we always tell each other everything," she admitted, looking down at her cup of tea.

"Yep, we always do," I agreed, feeling a moment of guilt because I hadn't always told her a hundred percent of everything.

A burning pinecone popped, causing me to jerk my head around.

"You look a bit nervous, Jo. Is anything wrong?"

"It's not me! It's you, Allie. I heard it in your voice. How do you know the woman in the picture—the woman who died?"

"You know I hate talking about my early years. I'm so blessed to live in this country…."

"Allie! Quit babbling, and tell me what's going on." I was ready to ring her neck. How could I help her if I didn't know what the problem was?

She took a sip of Earl Grey with milk, and then slowly set the cup down on the coffee table, looking more like a beautiful Hispanic robot than a real person.

The clock on the wall ticked, as pinecones snapped and popped in the carved stone fireplace.

Solow stood up, walked ten paces and stretched out on the carpet in front of the fire. Tansy curled up beside him.

After a pause, Alicia continued, "I probably told you I was the youngest of seven children, living with our mother in Tijuana, selling goods to tourists in order to buy food for the family. I was six years old when my new parents adopted me and brought me to California to live. They were in their fifties at the time and have both passed away."

I squirmed in my seat. I'd never met her parents, but I knew the story.

"Would you like more tea?"

"No, thank you," I sighed, "please, just keep talking."

"A few days ago my oldest brother, Del, and my youngest sister, Maria, contacted me from Mexico. But it's complicated."

"That's wonderful, Allie; why didn't you tell me before?"

"I guess I'm telling you now. I'd tried to find my family off and on for years, but didn't have enough information because I was only six when I left Mexico and my family had no official address in Tijuana…just cardboard walls and a piece of tin for the roof, like everyone else living on our side of town." Alicia's eyes looked glassy. She laughed nervously, "Now that I'm almost forty years old, I try to remember my family, but it's difficult."

"I can't even imagine," I said, thinking of myself at fifty, always surrounded and comforted by my Mom and Dad and Aunt Clara.

As if she were reading my mind, Alicia said, "And, Jo, I love your family and the way you include me in it. But sometimes I think about what it would be like to have my own brothers and sisters around me."

"How old is your brother?" I asked, feeling a selfish pang of sadness because I never had a brother, or a sister.

She thought for a moment, "I think Del is forty-seven and my sister was forty-one," her voice dissolved into sobs.

"Was? Oh, no…don't tell me," I whispered.

"Yes, the picture in the newscast was Maria, I'm sure of it. After I called you, I called the Sheriff and reported what I knew to be true. I'll be going to the Sheriff's Office tomorrow to answer questions. Actually, all I can tell them is her name and age. I don't even know Maria's birthdate."

"What about Del? Can't he tell them all about her?"

"I don't know how to contact him." Alicia said, as she gave in to one last sob and a couple residual hiccups. "He seems to be on the run."

My heart was breaking, but I needed to be strong for my friend. I turned my head away and wiped my eyes. "When was the last time you saw your brother and sister?"

"The first and last time I saw them was three days ago," she sniffed. "Del told me that he'd been working as an accountant for a rich family living near Ensenada. He had access to a computer and that's how he found my phone number and address."

"Sounds like it was their dream to find you."

"Maybe, but it's not all good. The three of us met at a coffee place in Watsonville. I wanted to tell you about it, Jo, but Del said that a very dangerous person was after them and they didn't want me or anyone else to become involved. Maria said they expected things would be better soon and then we could all be together. I gave them all the money I had in my wallet and a credit card. At first Del refused it, but Maria said it would be a loan."

"Were they in rags, broke, hungry?"

"No, quite the opposite. Maria had a lovely manicure, her jewelry was exquisite and her hair was nicely styled. Del's clothes looked tailored and expensive. In fact, they both looked a little over-dressed for Watsonville, except for the huaraches. Not many people wear leather sandals this time of year." She sniffed and focused on the ceiling for a moment. "Jo, I can't tell you how hard it was to let them leave. It was raining as I watched them run across the parking lot and jump into a white van." She wiped her eyes, and stared at the coffee table without seeing it.

"Can you think of anything that will help us find your brother?"

"They said they'd been living and working on a small island off the coast of Baja, but the license plate on the van wasn't from Baja."

"If they lived on an island, they probably didn't have a car," I said.

"Well, the license looked like it was from out-of-state, but I was too far away to see what state. It was light blue with something green in the middle."

I picked up Alicia's cell phone from the coffee table and handed it to her. "Google current American license plates, and start with the states closest to California."

Obediently she pulled up Washington, Oregon… "That's it! Oregon! I'm sure of it," Alicia said, pointing to a big green tree pictured in the middle of the plate.

"So it looks like they traveled up to Oregon from Ensenada, rented a van and drove down to California," I said, wondering if Del was currently hiding out in the redwood forests of Santa Cruz County, since Maria had been found in Felton. They wouldn't be the first or the last people to hide in the rugged mountains of the San Lorenzo Valley.

The ringing of Alicia's house phone crushed the uncomfortable silence.

I leaped up, grabbed the phone from the dining room and brought it back to Alicia. She looked at it like it was covered with germs. On the fifth ring she pulled herself together and answered. I sat next to her as she said to her husband, "Darling, Maria is…."

She handed me the phone.

"What was that about?" Ernie asked. "Who's Maria?"

"Alicia will tell you when you get home."

"That's the problem, we're trying to get out of Salinas, but the streets are flooded. We're parked in the Walmart parking lot. So far it's not flooded, and Trigger's okay. Looks like he's down for the night."

Alicia reached for the phone. "Honey, are you okay? How's Trigger?"

"Don't worry; he's asleep in the back seat. I'll stay here as long as it takes. But how are you and why is Josephine there?"

"Snap, crackle, pop."

"Phone's breaking up…we'll be home soo…."

Alicia's facial muscles relaxed a bit. She could postpone telling her husband about Maria, at least for a while. I decided I'd stay with her until Ernie and Trigger made it home. We popped popcorn and watched a movie on TV. Alicia stared at the screen, but I had a feeling she didn't see a thing. One of the strongest, bravest women I'd ever known had come undone. Her eyes had a faraway look as if she were remembering her childhood, her brothers and sisters and a mother who'd tried desperately to keep the family together even though they lived in the worst of slums.

Around midnight I heard noises and opened my eyes. The TV was still on, but the new noises I heard were the front door opening and closing and Ernie's footsteps as he guided a sleepy Trigger up to bed.

Alicia yawned, trudged across the living room carpet and headed upstairs to bed. She looked back at me and suggested I sleep on the couch. Solow and I were fine with that. The storm had let up, but I was too sleepy to drive home.

On my way back to the couch from a trip to the bathroom, I glanced out one of the windows facing Drew Lake and did a double-take when I thought I saw the moon reflected on the lawn. At least that was where the lawn had always been. It was late; maybe I was tired and confused. I curled up on the couch and pulled a lap blanket over my tired body while Solow slept like dog.

CHAPTER 2

Driving home Wednesday morning from Drew Lake, I reveled at intense sunlight glinting off a million rows of salad greens covering the valley floor from the city of Watsonville all the way south to Murphy's Hill in Aromas. Yesterday's dark stormy weather seemed like a long-ago nightmare. But weather wasn't the only nightmare that had clouded the air. I worried about Alicia and her stoic attitude. After a good night's sleep she'd become her old self again, strong and sure. She cheerfully served us breakfast and thanked me over and over for stopping by, as if I'd just popped in to borrow a cup of sugar. If there was ever an opposite of a "drama queen," it was Alicia. She'd already tucked her sorrow away.

Solow rode silently beside me, fat as a piglet full of mother's milk. He had a way of looking at people that made them want to share their food with him, and the Quintanas were no exception.

David had called me during breakfast and left a message. Instead of calling him back right away, I decided we'd simply stop by his house for a little visit. A bit of comfort and quality time with my stud-muffin would cheer me up, and Solow was very fond of David. I turned onto his long, paved driveway and noticed that his little Miata was not in its usual spot. I walked up to the garage and looked through the backdoor window. Only the Jeep was there. I went to the front door and rang the bell. No one answered. Maybe that was best, as I was still wearing my pajamas and slippers and my teeth and hair needed brushing.

"Okay, Solow, we're going home." I turned the key in the ignition and two minutes later we were chugging up my gravel driveway. I parked in front of the house and helped Solow out of his seat. We dodged a few puddles as we made our way to the front door.

Once inside, I ran the phone messages.

The first message was from David. "Josie, I'm at the Watsonville Hospital. Nothing serious. Seems I pulled a tendon in my left ankle when I slipped on the front porch step. They gave me a boot to wear and I should be home around two this afternoon. Would you mind letting Fluffy out? I forgot all about her."

The next message was from my Aunt Clara, just wishing me a happy Sunday and not to worry about the tree that came down in the storm. It missed the house and took out the tool shed.

The third and last message concerned my new mural project due to start Thursday morning. The contractor at the Felton Recreation Center said I'd have to hold off starting the mural until the following Monday. The newly plastered fourteen by thirty-foot wall needed one more coat of paint, but the undercoat was taking longer to dry than expected, due to the damp weather. One part of me was happy about the delay, the other part of me wanted to be in Felton painting and looking over the crime scene in my spare time.

Still thinking about Felton, I dashed out the door and down the driveway to fetch my newspaper. The headline read, "October Surprise." Splashed across the cover page was a picture of Maria. Suddenly tears for Alicia were all balled up in my throat. I felt her heartache, and hoped she'd never see the front page of the newspaper.

The story was even more poignant than the picture. Reportedly costumed kids and parents, riding in open-top train cars pulled by a well-preserved 1890's steam engine, looked down over the side of a train trestle. Since it was Halloween night, they weren't shocked to see what looked like a body stretched across the top of a boulder. The engineer yanked the whistle and people cheered as the train chugged three and a quarter miles down the wooded mountain, returning to Roaring Camp Station. Reportedly, there were shouts, giggles and compliments when the scary Halloween moon-light-ride ended. Even the engineer thought the lady on the rock was part of the annual spooky decorations set out along the narrow-gage tracks.

But not everyone believed she was fake.

The article said an unidentified person had called the police.

The small town of Felton was a lot like its neighboring towns. Driving north from Felton on Highway Nine, hugging the steep banks above the San Lorenzo River, first came Ben Lomond, then Boulder Creek. Each little town had a two-lane main street, one or two traffic lights, a fire station, grocery store, drug store, post office, a couple of antique stores, a school, a church and a few other one-story buildings. The towns were founded in the nineteenth century and many of the structures today are from that period. Marshall Dillon would have been comfortable in any one of the mountain towns, and the stagecoach robbers would have had so many places to hide in the surrounding forest.

Felton had something the other little burgs didn't, Henry Cowell State Park and Roaring Camp. It was almost impossible to tell where the park became Roaring Camp and the camp became the park. Conveniently, most visitors enjoyed both attractions in one trip. Sadly, now Roaring Camp had been stamped with the ugly fact that a murdered woman was found atop one of its boulders near its famous Roaring Camp Railroad. Most Feltoners hoped the sad news would be forgotten by the time summer tourist season arrived. But a few twisted optimists thought the news might actually be a tourist attraction.

My feelings ping-ponged from sadness for Alicia's loss, to curiosity about the strange accident and what the newspapers were now calling an "October Surprise." I rolled my eyes when I read how disturbed the business community was. They could afford to be disgruntled because it wasn't their family member who'd died. Once again my throat felt like I'd swallowed a golf ball. Poor Alicia.

"Okay, Solow, we'll walk over to David's place and let Fluffy out."

A few minutes later, Fluffy jetted out the front door, streaking across David's five acres of garden, orchard, oak trees and nicely mowed grass. Solow bounded along behind her. They headed next door to my five acres of tall grass, oak trees and a couple half-dead marigolds in the window box. I trudged along behind them. After some heavy panting and a quick rest on my back patio, Solow took another turn at chasing Fluffy. That didn't last long. Tongue lolling out one side of his mouth, Solow collapsed at my feet in front of the back door.

There was no lack of energy on Fluffy's part as she calmly circled the patio, swished her magnificent white tail at Solow, then sauntered back to her own home. If David and I had married years ago, would we have had a sweet little boy and one sassy little girl? My heart sped up at the thought of marriage. I loved David with all my heart, but marriage was a big step.

An obnoxious ringtone knocked me out of my reverie.

"Hi Aunt Clara."

"Josephine, dear, are you busy?" she asked.

"Not at all. Where are you?"

"I'm at home," she said, sounding less than her usual energetic self.

"Is something the matter? Where's Ben?"

"He's on a fishing trip in Mexico with a couple of friends. I didn't want to go and I'm sure they're happier without me. It's really a trip for the men."

"You sound like you need some company."

"Dear, it's nothing really; it's just that the place is so quiet when Ben's gone."

"Were you alone when the tree came down?" I asked.

"Yes…maybe it's just nerves. I'm just being silly."

"Auntie, I was feeling lonely before you called. I'll get David settled in and then come over to see you."

"Josephine, don't you have to get up early and go to work tomorrow morning?"

"Nope, I'm not working until Monday. Doug Davidson, the contractor, called and told me the wall didn't dry in time for a second coat of paint."

"Is that good or bad for you, dear?"

"It's good. I have a lot to tell you, Auntie. I'll bring barbecue for dinner."

We hung up and I headed into the bathroom for a quick shower.

My Aunt Clara lived with her retired building contractor husband, Ben, in a nicely renovated cabin surrounded by redwood forest north of Boulder Creek. It was a one-hour drive from my house if traffic was light, and about fifteen minutes coming from Felton.

The kitchen phone rang. I dashed for it, soaking wet and wrapped in a towel. It was David letting me know that he'd arrived safely home and thanking me for letting Fluffy out. I asked if he felt up to having company. From the sound of his voice, I could almost see his boyish grin over the phone, chocolate brown eyes twinkling, as snow white teeth appeared from behind kissable lips.

I brushed my teeth, dabbed perfume behind my ears and then ran a brush through my damp shoulder-length auburn hair. Solow recognized the routine and waited by the door. When I was finally finished primping, he happily marched on short springy legs across our two properties to David's back yard patio.

I caught up to Solow a couple minutes later.

A sliding glass door opened.

David leaned out. "Josie, are you here for a visit with the patient?" he smiled.

"Solow and I decided to go for a run, and your house got in the way," I bantered. By that time we were in a tight hug. I felt him teeter slightly. "Let's sit down before you fall down," I suggested.

"Don't worry, Josie. I'm really getting the hang of walking in this boot." He let himself fall back into an easy chair. "Is there something you wanted to tell me?"

"Yeah, there's a lot I need to tell you, but first I'm going to make a cup of tea and a ham sandwich for my poor patient."

"Hey, honey, you don't need to...."

"I know you can take care of yourself, but I won't see you for a day or two. Aunt Clara's home alone so I thought I'd go cheer her up."

"Cheer her up?" David laughed, "She's the most positive person I've ever known."

"Even Aunt Clara can have an off day. I just want to make sure you have everything you need before I go."

"Don't worry about me; I'll be fine," he said. "Give Clara my love when you see her."

It would have been easy for me to leave at that point, but I needed to tell David about Alicia's heartache. Halfway through the story, he said he'd seen the news about the mysterious woman found dead on a rock. Suddenly he looked devastated. We held each other until our sorrow subsided enough to let go.

A big part of me wanted to stay with David, but I sensed something was wrong at Clara's house and I'd already promised my aunt some good barbecued ribs. I was sure that Solow was just as torn between staying in Aromas and traveling to Boulder Creek. Once we were in the truck heading north, he settled into the passenger seat for his first nap of the day, oblivious to roadwork and heavy traffic. I wasn't worried about being late. No arrival time had been mentioned, just a barbecue dinner.

As we entered Felton, Solow barked at "nothing" under his breath. That usually meant he needed to pee. I made a sharp left and parked in the parking area for the Covered Bridge Park, a small family park featuring a covered bridge picturesque enough for a Currier and Ives print.

As soon as Solow's door opened, he leaped to the ground instead of waiting for me to help him down. The object of his eye was a waist-high, thick redwood post with a large metal ring attached near the top, obviously a place to secure one's horse, since it was situated next to the horse-bike-dog-people trail. When the post was sufficiently wetted down, I caught up to Solow and we walked the horse trail back toward my truck.

A wispy blond teenage girl passed by us, riding her dark silky Arabian. She and the horse were "one" as they skillfully maneuvered around dogs, children and the occasional biker. As they passed us, she slowed the horse, leaned down and asked my dog's name.

"His name's Solow," I said.

"Nice dog," she said.

"Thanks, nice horse. You might want to head back to the barn—big black clouds are coming this way."

"Thanks," she said, "I think the wind is picking up too."

Our next stop was the Barbecue Bunker and Bar, located on Central Avenue like every other business in Boulder Creek. Side streets were for homes and churches. Surrounded on all sides by deep green forested mountains, the little western-style logging town had barely changed its original look from a hundred and fifty years ago. Parts of the ubiquitous redwood forests had been logged up until recent times, but logging trucks were becoming extinct and the forest had made a huge come back. Sadly, good intensions and overgrowth had backfired and brought on nature's wrath. Many California forests had already burned and the rest were over-grown tinder boxes waiting for one spark to set them off.

We were two days into November, one day after a substantial rain storm, and the air smelled fresh following a long fiery Indian summer. Solow and I climbed down from our seats, stretched and sucked up the clean crisp air.

Solow peed on a hubcap.

"Did he have to do that?" an old gentleman snapped.

I smiled when he bent down gingerly to pet Solow's long sleek body.

"Sorry about that, but anointing your classic Vet could be considered a compliment. Solow knows his cars."

"Well, this is a sixty-two. Don't make 'um like that anymore," he laughed. "Name's Keg, but you can call me Keg," he snorted.

"I'm Josephine," I said, holding out my hand for a hand shake. His boney grip was less than firm, but his mind seemed pretty sharp as he quipped about one thing after another.

The wind picked up and a few drops of rain fell.

"Nice meetin' ya, Josephine. Gotta run this food home before it goes cold. My cat will never forgive me." His tall, lanky body folded itself into the Vet and the motor roared. Keg waved goodbye to us as I lifted Solow back into his seat. Once he was settled in, I marched into Orly's Barbecue Bunker establishment and ordered a barbecue combo big enough to serve as dinner and tomorrow's lunch.

As I carried my box of takeout to the truck, a sudden gust of wind threatened to send my precious dinner flying. I tightened my grip, set the box down carefully in the truck bed and pulled down the Snug Top bedcover. I checked my watch. It was four-thirty. It had started to rain and I had half an hour to get to Aunt Clara's house before the dark night arrived. Clara lived three miles north of Boulder Creek—three miles from the nearest streetlight, or light of any kind. Finding the right turnoff would be tricky at dusk, especially in the rain.

Big Basin Highway was a lonely stretch of curvy two-lane road. My truck tires bumped over a series of small branches and forest litter to the beat of Bon Jovi's, "Livin' on a Prayer." Gusty wind shook my little pickup truck like a rat in the jaws of a coyote, moving us sideways and off the pavement a few feet. I tugged on the wheel, pulling us toward the center line. More bumps. Mazda headlights projected trouble ahead. I slowed and swerved around a large tree limb just as a deer shot across the road. Its back hoof tapped my fender with a "clunk."

A spooky "Harry Potter" forest shivered and shook around us as we crept along, hugging the white line, searching for the proper turnoff. Finally, I recognized the entrance to the one laner I was looking for. The miserable little pot-holed road led to an unpaved driveway that curled, twisted and stretched up to the top of a forested mountain. With each new turn, I looked for lights from the house. To my surprise, my headlights suddenly lit up a low rock wall marking the end of the driveway.

Clara and Ben's house was just a dark featureless smudge on my right, until I pulled a flashlight from the glove box and aimed it at the front door. A piece of something, possibly a roof shingle, swished by, followed by what sounded like flying twigs smacking into my truck. I climbed out of my seat feeling like a freaky forest target and helped my reluctant dog to the ground. The wind pushed at our backs as Clara's door swung open. In that first moment, I saw a flickering candle with her pale face behind it, eyes wide and white hair tussled.

"Oh my! Come inside," she instructed. "I didn't think you'd actually come all this way in the storm."

I pulled the door shut behind us.

Aunt Clara and I hugged in the dark. I felt her shiver.

One set of bloodshot eyes appeared from somewhere in the house.

Aunt Clara's beloved Rottie, Sara, attacked Solow with her giant paws and her kisses. They sniffed and licked and played as if it were an ordinary sunny day in July.

"Auntie, it's so cold in here."

"I know, dear." I can't seem to find my flashlight so that I can find the wood, paper and matches to start a fire. The electricity has been off for a day and a half."

"It went off before yesterday's storm hit?"

"Yes, dear, you see the electric company shut the power off because of windy conditions."

"Auntie, I'll get the fire started. You go run a hot bath and get yourself warm."

"We don't have hot water."

"Okay, get in my truck and I'll run the heater. Your hands are freezing!" I walked her out to the truck, put it in neutral and cranked up the heater. My seventy-five year old aunt climbed stiffly into the passenger seat like an old woman. Normally she moved like a woman half her age. Her sister, Leola, my mother, was seventy-nine. Mom and Dad were still hiking up mountains, sailing, skating, bowling and a million other things. Typically, Aunt Clara used most of her energy pushing a vacuum cleaner, bathing Sara and helping me solve murder mysteries.

"Honk the horn when you're feeling toasty warm."

Clara nodded that she would.

Back in the house I focused on gathering paper, wood and matches. When the fire was finally set, I put a match to it but no flames appeared. I saw a pile of loose papers on the kitchen counter and figured the paper was there to start fires in the stove. Using one paper at a time, I was finally able to feel a little heat from a few timid little flames. The kindling eventually caught fire and smoke filled the room.

A horn honked.

Glad to leave the old cast iron stove and smoky kitchen behind, I hurried outside to my truck, turned the ignition off and helped Clara down from her seat. I followed her back into the house and watched her work the damper. Our coughing fits stopped when the air finally cleared. We rounded up and lit a scattering of candles, but dark shadows prevailed.

Half an hour later I took off my jacket.

Aunt Clara shed her heavy wool cardigan and fanned herself with a small book "Color This Day Beautiful," my favorite book of poems. It felt good to be warm, but I soon realized that the warmth only went so far. The living room was beginning to thaw, but the bedrooms were stone cold.

"I'm getting hungry," Aunt Clara complained.

Suddenly I remembered our takeout barbecue dinner in the truck bed. Cold rain water slapped my face as I raced out the back door and leaped over several puddles on my way to the back end of the truck. After a good fight with nature's fury, I presented Clara with a damp box of cold food. I transferred the meat and fries onto a cookie sheet and placed it on top of the wood stove to warm. The room filled with the heavenly scent of barbecue.

Sara and Solow milled around the large country kitchen, wide-eyed and panting.

"I'll give them some kibble," Clara said.

"Maybe we can top the kibble with barbecue juices from the bottom of the box," I suggested.

Suddenly there was a loud crash, the house shuddered and all the candles went out but one.

"Auntie, what was that?"

"I'm afraid I don't know, dear…"

CHAPTER 3

In one-millionth of a second, the sound of exploding glass coupled with a jarring thud had traveled from the living room to the kitchen where Clara and I were preparing to enjoy our reheated candlelight dinner.

Aunt Clara stood up for a second, a flickering candle in her steel grip, then fell back into her chair.

I grabbed the candle, and handed her my flashlight. "Are you all right, Auntie?"

"Don't worry," she waved me away.

"I'll be right back," I said, as I darted out of the kitchen and took a look at the living room. Wildly flickering candle light revealed the protruding crown of a giant redwood tree, dripping wet and completely out of place. If the tree had been three feet shorter, it would have landed without harm to the house. Cold, damp air quickly invaded the living room through the broken window.

I wheeled around and headed back into the kitchen.

"Auntie, we can't stay here. It's getting colder by the minute."

"But this is my home..."

"Okay, we'll eat this meal quickly, and then go to my house," I said, in the strongest, sternest voice I possessed. "The phones don't work and this wood stove isn't going to be enough to keep us warm with the window gone. And look, there's only one stick of wood left."

Like a zombie, my aunt dutifully ate her dinner.

After we ate, I helped Clara round up a pillow case full of clothing for the next few days while the dogs licked our paper plates clean.

We all hustled out to the truck.

Two feet from the passenger door, Aunt Clara stopped and stared.

"Where will we put Sara?" she muttered.

"Here, I'll pull the seat back…oh, it doesn't go very far. Just get in and I'll help Sara onto your lap. And hurry, we're getting soaked!"

"Oh dear…mercy me…golly gee," Clara groaned as she pulled herself up into the cab an inch at a time.

I opened the Snug Top on the truck bed and slipped Clara's bag of clothes inside.

"Auntie, shine the flashlight over here, against the house. I'm going to make a ramp out of this plywood."

"Ben makes the loveliest birdhouses using that wood."

"He won't mind if I use some of it, Auntie. Get ready for Sara."

Leaving her door open, I lined three bird houses against my truck and leaned a sheet of plywood on them. Then I tried to imagine a ninety-pound Rottweiler on Clara's lap. Soaked to the skin, I pulled Sara away from the back porch and up onto the slanted wood. After much pulling on Clara's part and pushing on mine, Sara finally decided to climb onto my aunt's lap.

"Solow, come!" I shouted, as I stood in a shallow puddle not even feeling the water around my ankles. The water quietly worked its way up my Levis, turning my knees into ice cubes.

Solow looked at the makeshift ramp.

"Solow, come!"

When that didn't work, I just grabbed him from behind and hoisted him into the cab. He quickly settled himself under the dash, but Clara looked miserable. I slammed her door, quickly disassembled the ramp and climbed into my seat. Sara's head rested on my lap.

The plan was to make a straight run for home.

The weather elves snickered. Even the wind whistled its doubts.

"Dear, did you know that your left headlight isn't working?"

"Yeah, but don't worry; I can see just fine," I said, with such calm assurance that I almost believed it wasn't a problem. After a few tight turn-around turns back and forth, we headed down the driveway to the bottom of the mountain and onto the Big Basin Highway.

The road was even more cluttered than the last time I'd seen it.

A utility truck and trailer full of tree limbs sat at the side of the road.

"How much longer, dear?"

"An hour if we're real lucky," I said. "Anything wrong?"

"Sara's scratching a flea. She has the pointiest elbows," she giggled.

"We can't stop now. How would we get everyone back into the truck?"

"I know, dear. We'll be fine," she said in a big brave voice.

The miles slipped away. Sara, Clara and Solow were in a contest to see who could snore the most creatively. My mind was on the road. If the other headlight went out, I might have mere seconds to react. We put Boulder Creek behind us, then Ben Lomond.

Downtown Felton came into view. I pulled to a stop at the four-way stoplight that wasn't working for lack of electricity. The entrance to Mt. Hermon and Graham Hill roads was closed—barricades and flares made the point. We'd have to continue on Highway Nine, curviest road in the county and a longer way home.

As we slowly left the eerily dark town of Felton, my headlight caught what seemed to be a person lying on the ground at the edge of the road near a yellow "Deer Crossing" sign. I slowed the truck. Was this a real person or just a prank? I couldn't just ignore him, so I parked the truck a few yards past the body and grabbed my flashlight from behind the seat. I circled the truck and stood aghast, staring at a man lying very still on wet spongey ground.

I checked for any on-coming headlights, but the highway was empty.

I heard a voice over the roar of the wind.

"Ola…"

I stepped closer to the man sprawled on the ground. Obviously he was alive, but was he dangerous? A million thoughts raced through my head.

"You're alive! Thank God!" I said.

"Ola. Yes, I am alive but I cannot move." The man was obviously in his forties, judging by his full head of black hair and strong voice. His wet clothing clung to a long, lean body. Why was he helplessly lying in mud? I circled the man, asking questions until I was sure he needed my help.

I checked my phone. It still wasn't getting service. There'd been no sign of life in Felton, so how could I help him?

"Please take me with you," he begged, as I pulled him up to a sitting position. The man instantly put a hand to his forehead.

"Your head's bleeding," I stammered, pointing the light at his forehead.

"Yes, that is true." He looked at my truck and scanned the dark night surrounding it. He had no way of knowing that the cab was already overstuffed with Clara and the dogs, but he took my word that all I could offer was a cluttered space under the Snug Top. With my help, he was finally able to stand. Together we took little steps over to the back of the truck. Even soaking wet, he smelled of wood smoke and aftershave.

A car—the only car so far—whizzed by us, splashing water our way.

The wounded man leaned against the truck while I pushed the Snug Top wide open and pulled the tailgate down. He bent over the tailgate and used his arms to crawl into a space usually reserved for paint supplies and ladders. Once he was settled with his head resting on Aunt Clara's bag of clothing, I asked if he wanted to go to a hospital.

"No, Senora, no!" And then he was still.

I asked again, "Where do you want to go?"

There was no response so I draped my jacket over his cold body, lifted the tailgate up and pulled the Snug Top down. As I squeezed my mature body into the cab, I prayed that the man was not critically injured and would have enough air to make it home. Concentrating on the road, still cluttered from the storm, I tried to smooth out the sharp turns as much as possible.

Aunt Clara didn't wake up until I parked the truck in front of my house.

"Oh, my," she yawned. "I had the strangest dream. There was an ax murderer chasing my sweet Sara, but he turned out to be the Mayor of Felton and he wanted to adopt my dog. Of course, I said, no. Ben said he'd think about it. I woke up feeling angry with Ben. That doesn't feel good. I need to call him."

"I thought you said you couldn't reach him."

"I can't when he's on the boat, but evenings are different because they're staying in a hotel."

I quickly set my seat in the far back position, opened my door and climbed out of the driver's seat. Reaching into the front seat, I tugged on Sara's collar and finally coaxed her into squeezing past the steering wheel. She jumped to the ground, giving Aunt Clara room to breathe.

Next, I opened the passenger door for Clara and gave her a hand as she climbed down from her seat. Solow jumped down to the driveway and trotted toward the house. The rain had stopped and silence prevailed. A silvery moon lit the way to the front door, but halfway there we heard a moan and whirled around in unison.

Sara's fur pointed straight up and Solow howled.

Clara paled as we watched the Snug Top rise up, seemingly on its own. I grabbed her arm in case she fainted and apologized for not telling her about the wounded man lying on her bag of clothes. The Snug Top was already at half-mast so I put the tailgate down and the man dangled his legs over the side.

"Can you stand up?" I asked, as he twisted his body around and slid to the ground.

30

Clara's eyes bugged, her mouth gaped.

The man groaned as he fell against the side of the truck. "I may be able to stand...but my head is spinning."

That wasn't the half of it. He was covered in mud and dead leaves that stuck to the mud like bug splats on a windshield. Dried blood on one side of his forehead and muddy shoes completed the picture of a man at his worst. Even with all of that, he was obviously handsome with white teeth and good manners. His perfect English came with a slight accent.

"Let's walk him up to the house," I said to my aunt. She positioned herself on his right and I held the man up from his left side. We walked him up three steps onto the front porch and leaned him against the house while I looked for the house key. The only time I locked the door was when Solow wasn't home. The rest of the time I didn't bother.

"Oops!" Clara said, straightening the man up and holding onto him with all her might.

I turned the key, the door opened and the three of us sidled through the doorway. We carefully dropped the man onto my couch, and I went about flipping various lights on, and then the furnace. Sara and Solow observed the man from a safe distance. I finished the chores while Clara brought a cup of water to the stranger. She pulled off his mud caked shoes and covered his cold bare feet with a lap blanket.

The gunky shoes ended up on the back patio.

The man was longer than my tweed couch but discomfort didn't keep him from falling into a sound sleep. I should have been concerned for his health, but mostly I thought about how much work it was going to take to shampoo and sanitize my sofa.

"Auntie, do you think he's comfortable?"

"Heaven only knows," she muttered. "Poor dear."

"Do you trust him?"

"Is there something about him that you don't trust?" she asked, as she cleaned the man's face with warm water and a washcloth.

"Well, we don't know him. What if he's an escaped ax murderer?"

Clara looked up at me. "You've been reading too many novels, my dear." She was probably right since I read mystery novels every chance I got. My mind automatically tried to fill in the blanks, like his profession and what he was doing that caused him to injure himself and how did he get such a serious wound on his forehead. I figured he was another clumsy hiker walking along the road at night in dark clothing. He was lucky he wasn't run over.

"Look at this…" Aunt Clara said, holding the man's hair away from his face.

I leaned closer. "Do you think it was a bullet that skimmed his forehead?" My voice quivered.

She nodded. "I'll finish cleaning and bandaging the wound, but I can't guarantee it won't get infected. We should take him to the hos…"

"No!" the man gasped. His head lolled to one side and then he was out cold again.

"Just in case, we should have David look at this wound," Clara said.

"I guess you're right, but I'll have to go get him. He has a bad ankle sprain." I hurried out to the truck, anxious to see my fiancé, but nervous about getting his opinion on the situation. I drove down my long gravel driveway, turned right onto Otis and three-hundred feet later, turned right onto David's paved driveway. His ranch-style home had a light in the kitchen window. I smiled in the dark as I made my way along the path to the front door.

I rang the bell.

Eventually David opened the door.

"Sorry, it takes me a while to get around," he laughed, pointing to a big black Velcro boot encasing his left leg up to the knee. "I thought you were going to Clara's for a visit."

"I did go, but their electricity had been turned off. And then a tree fell through a window. Her house was dark and freezing cold so I brought her home with me. I have something to show you. Would you mind coming with me?"

"I'm all yours, Josie, you know that," he grinned his irresistible grin, and followed me out to the truck. My Mazda pickup was a bit small for his six-foot-two body, but we managed. Two minutes and one long kiss later we left the truck and entered my house. David fussed over the two dogs briefly.

"Hello, David," Clara said, as she moved closer to him and they hugged. "We have a slight problem," she said, tilting her head toward the couch.

David looked down and studied the man for a moment. "Homeless?"

"We don't know," I said. "He was lying alongside Highway Nine in Felton. We couldn't just leave him there."

"Why didn't you call an ambulance or the fire department?" he asked.

"I tried, but the cell towers must have been out of power. My phone didn't work and the whole town was blacked out."

Clara held the man's jet black hair away from his injury. "What do you think?"

David leaned in for a closer look. "Could have been grazed by a bullet." He felt for a pulse on the man's neck. "He'll live," he pronounced.

Clara swabbed and disinfected the man's head before bandaging it.

David pulled the man's sleeve up. "Looks like he tangled with some poison oak and wild blackberry bushes recently." He held the man's right wrist up for Clara to see.

Aunt Clara cleaned the man's hands and forearms with soap and warm water. She smoothed on some salve and then tucked a lap blanket over the handsome stranger.

David cleared his throat. "If he's staying on the couch tonight, I'll sleep in your bed, Josie, and you can sleep in the loft with Aunt Clara." He said this knowing how small and lumpy the guest bed was. His proclamation appeared to be our punishment for bringing home a total stranger.

"I think we can trust him," Clara said. "If he wakes up in the night and sees Sara, he'll behave himself."

But in my dreams that night, a mysterious stranger morphed into an octopus. His tentacles were everywhere. When he sent a slimy limb down my throat, I woke up kicking and gagging.

Next to me, Aunt Clara slept on, confident the stranger was not to be feared.

CHAPTER 4

Thursday morning arrived with a crash.

My eyes popped open. It took a moment for me to remember why I was lying in Grandma's old coil-spring bed located in the loft above my living room. I leaped out of bed and raced down rickety stairs to the living room. The couch was empty. Following the sounds of conversation, I dashed into the kitchen where Clara was sweeping up at least a dozen broken pieces of pottery from what used to be my favorite vase. The contents of the dustpan clattered into the garbage.

Aunt Clara had already made coffee and toast for two handsome men sitting at my kitchen table, one bandaged and the other wearing a boot and a smile.

Boot and a smile stood up and said, "Good morning, Josie. I'm sorry I broke your vase. Guess I'm pretty clumsy wearing this boot."

A warm hug fixed everything.

"Good morning, Josephine, dear," Aunt Clara chimed in.

Mr. No-name ate his toast with relish—burnt as usual.

"Good morning, Mr....?" I said, sitting down at the table next to David.

"Poor soul can't remember his own name." Clara looked dour.

I looked past the bruises on his face, and stared squarely into the man's dark brown eyes. "What were you doing last night before we found you? Can you remember anything at all?"

He shook his head. "No, I can only remember today when I woke up on your sofa with two dogs staring at me."

Was he playing the old "amnesia card," I wondered?

"Is that David's robe you're wearing?"

"Yes, He has been most kind to me," he said, absently stroking one of my Disney mugs with his long fingers. He poured half-and-half and sugar into his steaming coffee refill, his jet black hair still damp from a recent shower. Last night's gauze and tape had been replaced with an ordinary flesh colored bandage. I breathed easier, confident the man wouldn't die of an infected wound while temporarily housed on my property. But I wasn't ready to trust him.

"Would you like another piece of toast, Roger?" Clara asked.

The man laughed and thanked Aunt Clara for naming him, Roger. She put a fresh batch of buttered toast on his plate and topped off his coffee with a few more drops.

As polite as Roger was, he shoveled food like he hadn't eaten in quite a while. He liked being called Roger and looked happy to have people around him. Or was he pretending to enjoy us and Clara's burnt toast and super strong coffee?

David took a last sip from his cup, then asked Roger if he'd like to go see his orchard. Roger said he'd like that very much. I watched from the kitchen window as the men trudged across our two properties, Roger still wearing a borrowed robe and slippers. David clunked along wearing yesterday's work clothes and one black boot.

We didn't see the men again until lunchtime when they came through my back door laughing and looking for sustenance. Roger came back wearing a pair of David's Levis, a button-down plaid shirt and a pair of Nike's. The men could easily have been mistaken for brothers as both were tall, slim, light brown complexioned with dark eyes and hair. Looking very distinguished with a few grey streaks in his hair, David was obviously a decade older than Roger.

"Josie, we're starving," David laughed, as he entered my kitchen.

Aunt Clara put down her book, and headed for the fridge. "How about soup and sandwiches? And Roger, don't you look smart in David's clothes!"

David and Roger offered to help Clara in the kitchen, so I excused myself and took the dogs for a walk. Otis Road didn't cut straight through my neighborhood; it curved this way and that past at least a dozen driveways. Each driveway led to a house on five acres. Some had a barn, some had a pool, some had an orchard like David's and some were just small unpretentious homes like mine. About halfway up the road, I noticed a green pickup truck with a California forestry seal on the door panel. The driver seemed to be dozing, his head turned away and resting against the seat.

The dogs let me know there was a stranger in the neighborhood with a bark and a howl.

We continued our walk to the end of the road. On our way back I noticed the pickup was gone. In the ten years I'd lived on Otis, I'd never seen a park ranger's truck in the area, probably because we didn't have a park or a river full of fish in our neighborhood.

The dogs followed me into the house, encouraged by the smell of tomato soup and grilled cheese sandwiches. I was the last to sit down at the table. Roger sat behind a full plate of gooey toasted sandwiches and a bowl of soup, not touching the food until I was settled into my chair at the table. He made the sign of the cross, and everyone began to eat.

"Roger, are you from around here?" I asked.

He chewed, swallowed and dabbed his lips with his napkin. "I don't think so…"

"Don't forget, dear, he has memory loss," Clara reminded me.

"We're just hoping you can remember something so we can figure out how to get you home," David said. "But in the meantime, you can stay at my house. I have two empty bedrooms and a whole box of clothes I've been meaning to drop off at the Salvation Army."

I noticed a couple quick blinks from Roger. Something in David's sentence meant something to him. To me, he was a puzzle to be figured out. David's offer was obviously intended to keep Roger from sleeping in my crowded little house. Obviously, there was some distrust on David's part.

My thoughts were interrupted when the house phone rang. I grabbed it on the second ring, said hello to Ben and handed the phone to Clara. Her voice sounded joyful as she walked into the living room, chatting away with her husband of less than a year. Finally, she came back to the table to finish eating her lunch, but she wasn't hungry—Ben was on his way to pick her up.

Ben arrived an hour later and took my sweet aunt and Sara home. With Aunt Clara gone, I decided to call Alicia to see what her day was like. I didn't mention Roger because Alicia tended to be overcautious like David and my mother. They didn't participate in spur-of-the-moment adventure. I never planned to, but things just came up. Like Roger. How were Clara and I supposed to handle the Roger situation, just leave him there in the mud? But when things went sideways I could always count on Mom, David and Alicia to help straighten them out. Dad was usually stuck in neutral, not one to get involved.

Alicia said she had some business in Santa Cruz, so I offered to keep her company and maybe we could stop and see Mom and Dad. She was always happy to see my folks.

I would be picking Alicia up in an hour so I still had time to check on the boys. Even though the morning sun was bright and the air almost warm, another storm was predicted for the next day. I found David shoveling and Roger hoeing in the orchard, creating trenches to keep the expected rain water from flooding David's property.

Solow napped nearby, happy to be where the action was.

Because Solow was happy to be spending his day with the men, I felt no guilt leaving Aromas by myself singing to old songs on the radio. San Juan Road was a breeze, no traffic, just farmland in various stages of growing lettuce, cabbage and berries. A few strawberry fields were under water but typically the water would drain away in a day or two.

A double yellow line down the middle of the road prevented me from scooting around a wide, slow-moving tractor. But that was okay. Ray Charles was singing, "Hit the Road, Jack," on the radio and I did my best to sing along, eventually arriving at the Quintana house in Watsonville.

As I pulled the truck to a stop on Drew Lake Road, my heart sank. There was a black wreath hanging on Alicia's front door. How easy it was for me to put another person's misery aside. My best friend had lost her sister, and my mind had been in ten other places all morning. I sat in silence for a moment and promised myself I'd try to be of help to her.

Alicia met me at the front door before I had time to ring the bell. She climbed into my truck and we headed for Santa Cruz.

"So what do you need to do in Santa Cruz, Allie?"

"I have a two o'clock appointment to talk to the mortician."

"Oh, I see. Will there be a funeral?"

Alicia looked straight ahead at the highway. "Yes, just a small get-together for the family—and you and David, of course."

"Is there anything I can do or bring?"

"Would you like to bring homemade cookies?" she said.

"Sure, of course, I can bring cookies. When is the funeral?"

"Sunday at four."

Ordinary talk had become laborious. What does one say to a best friend who just lost a sister? Small talk was just that, small, transparent, insignificant and useless. I wanted to say something that would lift her spirits, but the words were not there. As usual, Alicia saw the worry on my face and tried to cheer me up. Even though she was ten years younger, she was always "the mom."

I curbed the truck in front of the Mortuary in downtown Santa Cruz at a quarter to two. We climbed the grand front steps of a building that resembled the Parthenon, but on a smaller scale which was painted a bluish grey with white pillars. The grey changed intensity as various rouge clouds blocked and unblocked the sun. Leaves from a nearby maple flittered across the wide concrete stairs behind us.

41

Alicia shivered and pulled her jacket closed.

I held the door open for her.

We entered a spacious lobby full of ordinary, traditional, contemporary and outrageously decadent-looking coffins on display. Alicia studied them for a few minutes. "I'll probably buy that one," she said, pointing to a tasteful coffin without excessive bells, whistles and gold trim everywhere.

"Where will the funeral be held?" I asked.

"In the building behind this one. They do everything here, even cremation."

I sat on a fancy but uncomfortable wrought iron bench while Alicia discussed plans for the funeral. She came out of the conference room twenty minutes later with red eyes, but she forced a smile when she saw me.

"Everything okay?" I asked.

She nodded. "I'm signed up for the basics, a few flowers and a priest. I said no to so many things because I know almost nothing about Maria. I just wish my brother would contact me so I can invite him to the funeral. I should have heard from him by now."

"Maybe he's holed up somewhere. He did say someone was after them. Right?"

"Yes, that's right, and I'm scared to death for him," Alicia's voice trembled.

I pulled a tissue from a box of tissue strategically placed on a little table next to the bench. How many hundreds of people had sat and cried on that bench? Thinking that a distraction might help Alicia, I reminded her that we were going to go see my Mom and Dad. She smiled and pulled herself together. I don't think the folks even noticed that her eyes were red.

Mom and Dad still lived in the house I grew up in, in downtown Santa Cruz just a few blocks from the mortuary. Probably built in the thirties, their bungalow was in good repair. Their neighbor, Myrtle, saw us from her front window. She flew out of her house, straightened her wig and walked through Mom's front door behind Alicia and me.

"This is a wonderful surprise!" Mom said, running fingers through her chic and very short haircut. "So nice to see you, Alicia."

"Good to see you too, Leola," Alicia smiled bravely.

"Where's Dad?" I asked.

"He had a bowling tournament in Sacramento for the last three days. He'll be home later today."

"Judging by the way those boys have been bowling, get ready for some puffed up chests," Myrtle commented.

I knew Myrtle, the octogenarian gambler, pretty well. She'd probably put good money on Dad's team.

"So what brings you to town, dear?" Mom looked at each of us.

Before answering, I glanced at Alicia sitting across from me in Dad's recliner. Her expression was blank, so I didn't bring up the funeral. If she wanted people to know she'd tell them.

"Nothing special," I said to Mom, "just running errands."

"Not working on the October Surprise?" Myrtle asked, squinting her ancient eyeballs and tilting her head in disbelief.

"No, I'm not involved in that, although we'll be painting in Felton next week." I winked at her and she chuckled quietly.

"What's this about an October Surprise?" Mom asked.

Alicia quickly offered a partial explanation. "The expression comes from a headline and story in the *Sentinel* about the recent murder of a woman."

Mom rolled her eyes as if to say, "Here we go again." She was used to me tailing criminals and she never liked the idea. "Some people play cards," she looked at Myrtle, "and some people chase bad guys," she said, to anyone listening.

Alicia didn't explain further so I dropped the subject, leaving Myrtle with a quizzical look on her puffy white face. My friend and I were both holding back information. I still hadn't told anyone but David about the stranger Aunt Clara and I had picked up in Felton. After experiencing my fiancé's negative reaction, I preferred to keep it to myself. Mom and Alicia were always warning me to beware of hitchhikers, lock my doors, don't eat sugar, don't buy cabbage on Tuesdays, and on and on until I wanted to climb to the top of the Golden Gate Bridge just to irritate them.

Suddenly the front door opened and Bob thundered in, still wearing his shiny blue bowling shirt and a huge smile on his face. His buddy, Bruno, was right behind him wearing the same team uniform and toothy grin. They seemed happy to have an audience for their good news. After ten minutes of sitting on the couch telling somewhat exciting bowling stories, Bruno began to sweat. He unbuttoned his blue shirt revealing a t-shirt with a big picture of the Tasmanian devil wearing a tiara. The picture had everyone laughing, including Bruno.

"Have you folks seen the news today?" Bruno asked, "Besides our team being number one, that is."

"I didn't catch the news today," Myrtle admitted. "I fell asleep on the sofa." That was a big admission for an old woman who thrived on news and gossip.

"Yeah, well the news is…" Bruno began.

"Excuse me," Mom said, as she stood up and gave Bruno a pat on his boney shoulder. "Anyone like a hot toddy, eggnog or hot chocolate?" We took turns telling her our preferences. Dad followed Mom into the kitchen so that he could help with the drinks and give Mom a proper homecoming hug and kiss.

"So what's the big news, Bruno?" Myrtle asked, reminding me of a very old and hungry lioness at the Zoo's feeding time.

He sat up straight. "Remember the woman who fell out of the train Halloween night? Well, someone reported seeing her and some guy the day before in a white van with Oregon plates. The cops think the couple might be connected with a drug ring that operates between Mexico and Oregon." Bruno smiled and straightened his shiny blue shirt.

"That's it?" Myrtle asked.

"Oh yeah, and the cops said she wasn't alone the night she fell out'a the train. Witnesses said there was a tall, well-dressed man with her when she climbed aboard. Another man sat down with them and they were all speaking Spanish." Bruno rolled his eyes to the ceiling. "Foreigners!"

Alicia stared at her hands which were carefully folded on her lap.

That was when I knew it was time to go.

Halfway home, I pulled my truck to a stop at the Doggie Diner. We ordered dogs and fries to go. Back in the cab, we ate and talked about silly things, skirting around Maria's death for the millionth time even though Bruno's words were fresh on our minds.

CHAPTER 5

Early Friday morning I leaped out of bed and tore down the hall, catching the kitchen phone on the fourth ring. It was Doug Davidson calling to say that the second coat of paint had been applied and he was pretty sure it would be dry by Monday. I took that as good news since I hadn't brought home a paycheck in the last two weeks.

Since I was already up, I decided to call Aunt Clara. Her phone rang several times.

"Hello...oh, Josephine, it's you. You're up early."

"Hi, Auntie, I just wanted to know if you have electricity yet."

"Oh my; it came on in the middle of the night. Several lights and a radio woke us up," she giggled.

"Is the house warm now?"

"To tell you the truth we're keeping warm in our bed. Brrr! I need to get back to Ben, I mean back to bed. Love you, dear." She hung up.

I smiled at the thought of Clara and Ben cuddled together keeping warm. Solow stood patiently at the back door so I let him out. My next stop was a warm shower and my warmest clothes. Many winters in the past had been mild, but this one was proving to be on the cold, wet side. The weather girl on KPUT TV said it would start raining Sunday and might snow at higher elevations.

After throwing a load of sheets and towels into the washing machine situated on the backyard patio, I treated myself to a delicious veggie omelet with two strips of bacon. I tossed the last couple of bites of omelet to Solow and then cleaned the floor where he'd created a puddle of drool.

It was still early, only eight o'clock in the morning, so I decided to review my sketches and plans for the Felton Rec Hall. The sketches were minimal, not much detail, just placement of the main items such as the train, depot, a few old west buildings and a large meadow ringed by redwood trees. We'd add more subjects as the work progressed.

David called. He wanted to know if he could borrow a shovel. Of course, he could. All I had to do was dig it out of my back yard shed. Solow followed me out to the old rusted refuge for paint, garden tools and a large community of spiders. As soon as I found the shovel, we hauled it over to David's orchard and handed it to Roger who wanted to get busy digging trenches right away.

David looked up from his excavation work. "Thanks, Josie, we need to finish this before the rain starts again." Roger was already digging in and tossing dirt, adding to one of several long diversion barriers designed to prevent root rot. Apparently, the trees like water but can be harmed by too much of it.

David walked up to me, his rubber boots sucking up one at a time from the mud. He wiped his forehead with the back of his hand. "Maybe I should let the water fill all the gopher holes," he said, in his most evil sounding voice.

"Yeah, give them a little swimming lesson and off they go," I laughed.

"But I want them to drown."

"With your nemesis' gone, what would you do all day?" I asked.

"I'd come over to see you," he winked.

"And if I know you're coming, I'll bake a cake. I see you're not wearing your black boot today."

"Can't. It won't fit inside the rubber boots. Actually, my ankle isn't so bad today," he said, wincing as he threw another shovel of mud.

"By the way, dinner's at six." I wished the men good luck and headed for home. Fluffy watched us from her perch at the top of a moss-covered fence post, while Solow ignored her.

Back home, I checked my washing machine, threw the wet contents into the dryer and turned it on. I heard the phone ringing inside the house so I quickly stepped into the kitchen and picked up the receiver. Too late, but the caller had left a message.

"Like, this is the Doggie Diner and we found a personal belonging of yours, so call us at le-ka-to-gum snap-de-de-pi-ba." I immediately opened my purse and checked the contents. Everything was there except the most important item, my wallet, which meant I'd be driving without a license, money and credit card.

I called Alicia. She picked up on the third ring.

"Hi, Allie; can you drive me to Aptos? It seems I left my wallet at the Doggie Diner yesterday."

"Sure, I need something to do. I reorganized two closets and painted the back shed. I just started organizing my sock drawer...again. Can't wait to start our next mural."

Poor Alicia. I'd never heard her sound so distraught. Maybe Solow could cheer her up. It was worth a try. We arrived in Watsonville after I nervously drove under the speed limit, knowing I didn't have my license with me. Not wishing to push my luck, I let Alicia drive us to Aptos. We clambered into her Volvo SUV and stopped at the diner ten minutes later.

The girl behind the counter put down her soda and snapped her gum.

"Can I help you, ma'am?" Oh, how I hated to hear that, "ma'am" word.

"Yes, well, you called me this morning to tell me that I left my wallet…"

"I didn't say *wallet*."

"Right, but since it's missing…"

"Ma'am, can you, like, describe the wallet?"

"It's black with little silver snaps."

"What's in it?"

"Money, credit cards, a picture of my dog."

Alicia looked at me funny. "Solow? Not David?"

I shrugged. "I meant to put one in there, just didn't get around to it."

The girl snapped her gum and handed over the wallet. I quickly checked to see if the important things were still there. They were, so I ordered three dippy dogs, each with dipping sauce and a crusty bun. We ate the dogs and drank our iced tea inside the establishment.

Solow ate his in the back seat of Alicia's SUV, then licked the leather seat clean.

"Does this make Solow a cannibal?" I asked.

"What, a dog eating a hot dog?" Alicia laughed her first laugh all day.

I cranked my head around to look at Solow. "Nice job cleaning the upholstery, old boy. I think he likes the taste of leather."

"They're nice seats, aren't they? I wish I could've taken my brother and sister for a ride." Her voice drifted away as her eyes tracked a family of four crossing the parking lot.

"Okay, time to head home, unless you have other stops to make," I said.

"Actually, I do have one stop. I'd like to have a jeweler look at Maria's ring. I think it's a fake, but we'll see." She pulled a diamond ring from her purse. The diamond was large, oblong and ringed with little rubies.

I glanced at my engagement ring, remembered David's smile when he presented it to me, and quickly decided that size was not important.

Alicia drove half a mile across Aptos and parked in front of the jewelry store. As we entered, a well-dressed gentleman greeted us and listened to her request. He pointed us to an office at the back of the store where a woman wearing magnification headgear sat at her workspace. They talked while I cruised the display cases.

Minutes later, Alicia stood beside me wearing a dumb-founded expression.

"It's real," she whispered. "Three carats!" Alicia didn't mention any more stops; she just drove straight home like an exhausted homing pigeon. I helped Solow climb down from the back seat, thanked Alicia for driving and hugged her tight.

"You'll feel better. Give it some time," I said, "and be sure you put that ring in a safe place."

Solow and I settled into the truck and watched Alicia enter the house before driving away. He fell asleep immediately like a good basset. From there, I drove over to the local grocery store where my young friend, Robert, worked. He happened to be pushing a train of carts across the parking lot and stopped at the truck to pet Solow.

I rolled the window down.

"Sleeps a lot?" he asked.

"Whenever he gets a chance. How are things with you, Robert?"

A gust of wind lifted his over-sized blue apron. He shivered. "Some winter we're having, and what a terrible Halloween with that murder in Felton."

"Yeah, this one has hit close to home. It was my best friend's sister who was murdered."

"Jeez, that's too bad. I read that she was from Mexico."

"That's right, and Alicia only saw her once since they were little kids...so sad."

"I know Alicia Quintana. That's too bad she lost her sister. Actually, the picture in the paper of the murdered woman looked a lot like Alicia."

"Robert, you have a good brain for solving mysteries. Why would Maria and her brother take a train ride up the mountain, at an amusement park, on Halloween night if they were running away from someone?"

"So she was with her brother?"

I nodded.

"And someone was after them?"

"Yeah, pretty crazy!"

"Maybe someone forced them onto the train with a Taser gun or something," Robert said, as I opened the door, slid down from my seat and changed the subject.

"Robert, I'm having people over for dinner tonight. Any suggestions in the way of comfort food?"

"How about a nice lasagna?"

"Spaghetti and meatballs would be easier. That's what I'll do."

Robert turned and continued his work, shoving a dozen carts toward the cart coral. Minutes later, we bumped into each other in the produce department where he gave me a couple of grapes to taste. I placed a bag of grapes and a bunch of broccoli in my cart next to the meat and spaghetti noodles. I tossed in a bag of Solow's kibble, a half a gallon of milk, a loaf of bread and a tub of ice cream. Robert rang up my groceries and helped me carry them to the truck. I arranged the bags in the bed and pulled the Snug Top down.

Robert stepped over to the passenger window. "Jo, I know you're getting involved in this murder. Just be careful," he said, giving Solow an ear rub through the open window.

"Thanks, Robert, I'll try."

I turned the ignition key and we headed for home. After a few miles, I noticed a green pickup following us through town and then onto San Juan Road. It reminded me of the truck I'd seen the last time I took Solow for a walk. The truck disappeared from view once I turned onto Otis. At that point, my mind quickly bounced over to dinner preparation chores.

At six o'clock sharp, David and Roger arrived in clean clothes, smelling like Ivory soap and after shave. They brought me a bottle of wine, a bag of corn chips and a pint of David's homemade apricot salsa. Dinner was pretty good, I think, and the whole evening quite pleasant. The three of us cleaned the kitchen in record time. Roger seemed like a family member, enjoying the simple things in life like old sitcom reruns. The boys were really into the sitcoms when they weren't watching football.

My mind was elsewhere. I was riding a train with three Spanish speaking people on Halloween night. *How and why did all that happen?* I asked myself over and over.

It had been dark for hours when I remembered I hadn't collected the mail. Solow needed a walk, so I grabbed a flashlight and took him down the driveway to the mailbox. Wind whistled in the branches of an oak tree and rainwater gurgled through a giant pipe under the driveway.

Solow left me and lumbered back to the house.

Feeling spooked, I ran my flashlight in a broad circle hitting everything in range including a green pickup across the street. A cold chill traveled from my neck down to my feet. I grabbed the mail, slammed the box shut and hurried up the driveway. Solow joined me at the front porch and we stepped inside the house.

"David, do you know anyone who drives a green pickup truck?"

He turned away from the sitcom and shook his head.

"Well, I keep seeing this truck…"

"How do you know it's always the same truck?"

Roger turned the volume down on the TV.

"I know it's the same one because it has a California ranger emblem on the door."

"Oh, you're probably right. I don't know anyone like that," David said, turning back to his program, his booted foot resting on the ottoman. He and Roger laughed in unison at the next punch-line. Maybe they really were brothers in another life. Even the part in their hair was in the same place on the same side. They acted like they'd known each other forever.

David pointed to the screen, "Roger, did you ever own a car like that?" he laughed. The TV car belonged to a teenager. It was old, noisy and clearly unreliable. Roger shook his head, saying that his teen years were nothing like David's.

"Can you remember growing up?" David asked him.

"Not really," Roger said, "but I sense that we were poor. I don't know how I know that."

"Maybe the rest will come to you when you least expect it," David patted him on the back.

By that time, I was ninety percent convinced Roger had lost his memory, but ten percent of me wasn't completely convinced. He had read the newspaper that morning, so he hadn't forgotten how to read. He bowed his head and said a prayer at dinner. He hadn't forgotten how to do that. I tried to learn from Aunt Clara's patience. Her way of dealing with the problem was to not press the man, using a sympathetic wait–and–see attitude. David didn't ask Roger for anything, but he did make an appointment for the mystery man to see his doctor.

Over and over, Roger promised to pay David back for food, lodging and the coming doctor visit. David said he wouldn't take Roger's money even if he had some. My fiancé had recently retired from IBM at age fifty-two. Even with a divorce in his past, David had managed his investments well. I knew he'd never take money from a down–and–out person.

Judging by Roger's perfectly manicured fingernails and the soft skin of his hands, he wasn't used to physical work. But he'd advised David on how to treat and prevent diseases in various types of fruit trees, including apricot and pear. He talked about amendments to the soil, the effects of temperature changes and demonstrated various pruning techniques.

David introduced Roger to his favorite types of music, classic movies and shared his recipe for apricot salsa. He told me he'd taken Roger to Walmart where the mystery man blinked and gaped in disbelief. Obviously, the man had never been in such a large store before.

David let Roger drive his Jeep around the property. He knew immediately how to operate it. He was also comfortable driving David's riding mower. Another of his interests was the *Wall Street Journal*.

David confided in me that even though Roger kept busy, he seemed to be depressed. We tried everything from old Lucy and Desi reruns to standup comedy skits and the newspaper funnies. Nothing worked.

Later that night, I fell asleep on the couch and dreamed about David and Roger participating in a drag race. They lined up at one end of Otis and raced four blocks to the other end. At the end of the road was a lake full of black swans and blue serpents. I tried to keep the men away from the lake by waving and shouting, but no sound came out of my mouth. David's mower and Roger's Jeep drove into the lake. I noticed there was an island in the middle of the water and the boys were headed there. Just before they reached the island, they both sank. Bubbles marked the spot.

CHAPTER 6

Weekends for me were like big platters of pastries just waiting for me to indulge, and I didn't want to waste a single moment. Saturday morning I was looking at forty-eight hours of free time before my mural job was scheduled to start, but I had to attend to necessary chores first. Solow was due for his vaccination and my truck needed a headlight bulb. The feed store in Soquel held a vaccination clinic in the parking lot on Saturdays and my favorite auto supply store was right around the corner.

A nice kid at the auto supply replaced the burnt-out headlight and Solow got a shot in his thigh which seemed to hurt me more than it hurt him. Once my errands were done, I decided to continue driving north and look around Roaring Camp. I'd been to the park a few times in my life, even wrote a paper on it in the sixth grade, but this time I'd be checking out a crime scene.

Bear Mountain monopolized the eastern side of Roaring Camp where hikers, bikers, horseback riders and a narrow-gauge locomotive all climbed three and a quarter miles to the top, looped and came back down. Number one engine—Dixiana—was one of three turn-of-the-century engines designated as National Mechanical Engineering Historical Landmarks.

The park owned a fleet of antiquated steam engines. A designated locomotive, usually Dixiana, made one run up the mountain at twelve-thirty every day except Christmas. The engine pulled six open-air cars, carrying tourists, into a lush forest and back again. Halloween night was the only schedule exception.

Entering Cowell State Park from Highway Nine, I drove half a mile south along a two-lane park road toward the main entrance. Off to my right was a large meadow partially ringed in Redwoods. Beyond that, stood a string of cottonwood trees lining a raging river heading toward Santa Cruz and the Pacific Ocean.

I slowed the truck so I could take it all in.

A wide footpath paralleled the road. I did a double-take when I recognized a beautiful Arabian horse prancing along the path with a rider wearing her black riding helmet, blond hair streaming down her back. Behind the dark horse was a dark-haired girl riding a lovely palomino. The first rider looked our way and smiled when she saw Solow's head hanging out the window.

The scene was surreal—too beautiful to be true. The riders disappeared behind a wall of trees right about the time I pulled up to a toll booth. I handed the ranger my credit card, he swiped it and handed it back with a receipt to be placed on my dash. I continued on the road as it wound through shady forested areas and ended at the tourist parking lot beside a museum and the park's Nature Store.

My stomach rumbled. It was noon.

I pulled to a stop in one of the few remaining empty parking spaces, stuffed some cash into my pocket, helped Solow down from his seat and hooked a leash to his collar. We followed the crowds up a wide path and over the railroad tracks to the depot ticket window. People were standing in line to buy tickets so I planted myself at the end of the line and worked my way toward the lady in the window. Naturally, the once-a-day train was scheduled for twelve-thirty.

A train whistle echoed across the 1880's life-size replica of an old western town. The haunting noise sounded like it came from far away. I'd taken the ride as a child but needed to see Bear Mountain again in light of the recent murder.

Minutes later, the whistle sounded closer and louder.

Serving as the last in line, Solow and I inched forward.

Two people were ahead of me.

A distinguished looking man dressed as a cowboy-sheriff zigzagged his white prancing horse down the tracks, clearing tourists off the rails, just before the train pulled to a complete stop and dramatically discharged copious amounts of steam. Children squealed as parents herded them toward favored train cars—three open-air and three with tent ceilings for protection from sun and rain.

Just as I was about to step up to the ticket window, a family with four little boys walked by. The boys stopped and glommed onto Solow, petting everything he owned. I could tell my buddy was uncomfortable, especially when the youngest boy lifted Solow's ear and placed a gummy bear in it. I bent down to help deflect the unwanted attention. The parents finally looked back and instructed their herd to hurry up or they'd miss the train. The boys quickly trotted down the boardwalk to join their parents, the littlest one coming in last.

Letting go of Solow, I raised up and turned back to the ticket window. It was closed. I banged my knuckles on the glass, but no one arrived to sell me a ticket. I circled the station, but found no one to help me. Even the cowboy was gone, and the train had started to move forward. I watched it leave the station with two long toots of the whistle. People waved to no one in particular as the train gained a little speed.

Did anyone care that I wanted a ride but was unable to buy a ticket?

Feeling a little sorry for myself, Solow and I wandered across the unpaved middle-of-town thoroughfare to the General Store. The place was very quiet, since most people were out enjoying a train ride to the top of Bear Mountain. I bought a piece of jerky and told the cashier what had happened to spoil my train trip. She was a jolly, short, plumpish woman with greying hair and a name tag that read, "D. Winkle." She explained that only working dogs were allowed in the store, but my adorable hound could come inside since business was slow.

D. Winkle wore a blue prairie bonnet and a long calico dress as her frontier woman costume. I was curious about a pinky ring she wore on her left hand. The center stone was pink, set in an ornate gold setting and surrounded by little fake diamonds. *Pretty flashy for a frontier get-up*, I thought.

We chatted and laughed at situations similar to my missing the train and all kinds of things she'd encountered in her years of working at the park. She regarded Maria's death as the worst thing that had ever happened. I asked her if she saw the woman who was murdered. Ms. Winkle said, "No," grabbed a feather duster and waved it over the counter like a nervous habit.

"That's a lovely ring you're wearing," I said.

"Oh, that." She put the duster down. "It doesn't even go with my outfit," she said, as her cheeks reddened.

A woman and her grandson walked up to the counter asking for help sizing a little feathered Indian bonnet for the boy. I roamed the store and ended up flipping through various books for sale. Most of them fell into the "train" genre. One train book had a map of Roaring Camp and Bear Mountain. I carried the book over to my new friend at the counter just as the little boy ran out the door wearing a round of feathers atop his curls.

"So what can I do ya for?" D. Winkle smiled, eyeing the book.

"I don't really need the book, but I was wondering if you could make a copy of this map?" I opened the book and showed it to her.

"Oh silly me, I have just the thing for you," she giggled and plucked one of the folded maps from a display case behind the counter. I left the store with a map in hand and most of my money still in my pocket.

Out in the bright light of early afternoon I sat on a bench and opened the little map of the park. The train schedule was printed in the lower corner plain and simple: train leaves at 12:30 every day but Christmas. With no chance of catching another train, I looked at the map to see if there were hiking trails. I found a bike trail that snaked up the mountain, a couple of winding walking trails and a fire trail that cut out most of the snaking and winding. All we had to do was follow the railroad tracks until we came to a junction with the fire trail.

Solow and I indulged in a burger and a cup of water before we began our trek. Walking along the railroad tracks, we left everything behind, tourists, hikers and all manner of noise. The mighty forest closed in on us. Three deer congregated a few yards ahead. Solow quickly pushed forward only to have his leash tighten. He bounced along on springy legs, always looking for wildlife. I looked too because I'd heard stories of cougars in the area.

Coming around a gentle turn in the tracks, we saw a paved road heading off to our left. It seemed barely wide enough for one vehicle, but had a nice surface for walking. About ten minutes later the gentle slope became a steep challenge. Jay birds mocked us as we struggled uphill, one leg at a time. Poor Solow had lost his usual bounce and walked slower and slower.

A far away train whistle fed my determination to reach the top. We didn't need the train—we'd get there on our own. And we did. After a good painful stretch of the legs, we finally arrived at the top of the mountain where there was a limited view because of the trees in every direction. Various forms of vegetation, including beautiful ferns, covered much of the ground. Passing clouds controlled the intensity of green that ranged from patches of fluorescent yellow-green moss to dark hooker's green in the shadows.

Desirous of a better view, we climbed up onto a six-foot by six-foot lookout structure made of concrete with iron railings on three sides. As we stood looking out across our tree-covered mountain and over to the next wooded range, Solow turned his head.

A clipity clop, clipity clop, noise became louder.

We heard a couple of whinnies.

Solow sniffed the air and wagged his tail.

Three riders on horseback trotted single file up over the ridge and stopped behind the lookout we were on. I recognized the first horseman as the Roaring Camp Sheriff riding his white horse. A dark Arabian horse and rider sidled up to the first. A palomino stood behind them swishing his long silky tail.

The blond rider eyed Solow and smiled.

"Good afternoon, ma'am," the cowboy said. "You might want to take the walking trail going back down. It's not as steep."

"Yeah, thanks, that's a good idea," I said, picturing in my mind Solow and me sliding down the paved fire trail on our butts or even worse, rolling down.

The man was easy on the eyes in his black mustache and white hair showing under a black Stetson. He looked pretty fit, possibly in his sixties. He pulled on his reins and backed his horse up, then took off down the trail he'd pointed out to me.

"Do you girls live around here?" I asked.

"Ben Lomond," the blond said; "he's my grandpa."

"He looks too young to be a grandpa."

"He's almost seventy." She smiled, obviously proud of him.

"That's a beautiful bracelet you're wearing."

"Yeah, but I'm sure it's fake. I found it near the trestle last week."

The dark-haired girl made a clicking sound with her tongue and pulled on the reins, turning her golden horse toward the walking trail. The Arabian followed. Blondie turned in her saddle to wave goodbye, her jeweled bracelet catching and reflecting sunlight.

After a few more minutes of communing with nature, Solow and I headed down the trail. A couple guys riding mountain bikes passed by us on their way up. The rest of the hike was quiet and easy walking as I let gravity do the work. About twenty minutes later, we arrived in downtown Roaring Camp which was filled with passengers from the recent train ride. We walked up to an outdoor blacksmith shop where the smithy stood by his fire demonstrating the making of horseshoes. The well-behaved Palomino and Arabian, tied at the hitching rail, seemed unconcerned with the demonstration. The two girls chatted with each other, mostly ignoring the smithy and his speech about pounding iron.

Not wanting to bother the girls, I stayed at the back of the crowd, but Solow squeezed his way through a cluster of people and went straight to them. They looked around to make sure I was near, since my dog was dragging his leash. Blondie raised her hand for a tiny wave to let me know that Solow was safe with her. From my vantage spot, looking through a maze of pant legs and small children, I watched Blondie gently massage Solow's back and head. He looked mesmerized, or at least in love.

Finally, the smithy quit talking and pounding iron, and the assembled group broke up. The two teenage girls walked Solow over to me and gave me their names—Liz and Grace. I introduced myself and asked if I could have a closer look at the bracelet. Grace held her wrist out to me.

"Would you be willing to sell..."

"No, but you can have it. Like I said, everyone says it's not real." She slipped it off her slender wrist and handed it to me. The bracelet felt heavy in my hand. I slipped it into my pocket and tried to hand Grace a ten dollar bill, but she turned away and said, "That's okay."

"Wait a minute."

Grace turned back.

"Can you tell me exactly where you found the bracelet?"

She looked like she wanted to roll her teenage eyes, but out of respect for older folks she said, "Under the trestle…the one you walked by today."

"So that's about ten minutes up the trail, would you say?"

"Yeah, something like that. It was on the ground where the big boulders are, near the little albino redwood tree." She looked at her friend. "I gotta go, sorry. We have chores to do and stalls to muck." She and Liz walked over to their horses and untied them.

I pulled on Solow's leash, then I pulled again. I knew he was tuckered out, but I wanted to see the albino tree that Grace had mentioned. Once the girls rode away, I was able to get him moving along the trail.

After about ten minutes of fast walking, I was able to see the train trestle in the distance. The redwoods had thinned out and there were large patches of open ground covered in grass. Near the trestle on our left was a scattering of large rocks and boulders, one tall redwood tree, and one delicate little redwood with pale whitish needles.

About twenty yards away, a couple of little boys were climbing on one of the huge rocks, the one with yellow crime tape stretched around it.

I walked up to them. "Sorry, boys, this is a crime scene." All three of us looked around for the parents who were about a hundred feet away sitting on a giant boulder in deep discussion. I shooed the boys away and began searching the ground for anything suspicious. I walked slowly in ever widening circles until I was touching the little "Charlie Brown" albino tree. Nothing sparkled anywhere.

Looking around the area, I saw more boulders and began checking around each one of them but found nothing. If the bracelet

Grace had found had belonged to Maria, how did it get so far away from the body? Unless the bracelet belonged to someone else? I scratched my head.

Solow whined. He generally wasn't a whiner.

In my mind I concluded that a person falling from a train crossing the trestle could conceivably land on a rock below. But how did the bracelet get twenty yards away? Did the clasp open by itself, allowing it to be flung in a different direction?

Once I was satisfied I'd seen all there was to see, I turned around and looked to the West. The sun was about to set and it would be dark soon. Solow's dinner clock had already gone off. He bounced along beside me like the hungry basset he was. By the time we reached the parking lot, the place was empty except for my truck and three park ranger pickups lined up near the entrance to the picnic area.

Stars were beginning to show themselves across a purple sky as we climbed into my pickup. I should have been satisfied with my snooping efforts, but I wasn't. Way too many pieces of the puzzle were still missing.

CHAPTER 7

The second half of the weekend started off with breakfast at my house. We'd pancakes and a bacon and spinach quiche baked by my guest, David, and eaten mainly by Roger, my other guest. We were celebrating the fact that David didn't need to wear his black boot anymore. Sitting at the table long after the food was gone, just drinking coffee and discussing gopher abatement, Roger seemed to be less than excited about that particular subject and excused himself to go check the ditches since it was already raining pretty hard.

"That worked pretty well," David winked.

"That's gopher talk for ya," I laughed. "Hey good lookin, how would you like to help me turn the mattress in the loft?"

"I'm all yours," he grinned.

He followed me up the hundred-year-old wooden stairs to my loft full of Grandma's old furniture. It was nice to finally be alone with David—so nice that we didn't come downstairs for almost an hour, not until he remembered he needed to call his son. Harley and his five-year-old daughter lived in Sacramento and were planning a visit. Would they arrive in time for dinner? In my experience, they probably wouldn't since Harley operated by the "seat of his pants" in most cases.

As I thought about Harley and sweet little redheaded Monica, I suddenly remembered I was going to a funeral at four o'clock and needed to make cookies!

A quick kiss and David and Solow were out the back door.

I checked the kitchen for cookie ingredients. My search narrowed the choices down to peanut butter cookies. Falling into my Rachael Ray demeanor, I mixed ingredients, formed the batter into walnut-sized balls, placed them on a cookie sheet and flattened each ball with a fork, leaving the traditional crisscross imprint. I pushed the cookie sheet into my preheated oven and set the timer.

The kitchen phone rang. I answered.

"Hi, Jo. Are you coming to the, ah…are you coming today at four?"

"Of course, I'm coming, Allie. How are you feeling today?"

"I'm not sure. I'm usually pretty organized…" she muttered.

"Don't worry about stuff, just get through the day and you'll be better tomorrow," I said, speaking from past experience when my grandmother died. It had been a well-attended funeral and I was her only grandchild. I was thirty-two years old at the time, and expected to get up and say a few words. My sorrow was deep, but my words came out like a pat Hallmark card. For years I'd regretted not saying what I really felt. Why couldn't I be like my Aunt Clara? Her words had been truthful, mournful, but uplifting and straight from her heart. Mom and her sister were straight shooters.

"Thanks, Jo. I'll make another cup of tea and see if that helps."

"What kind of tea?"

"It's chamomile tea."

"You might want to switch over to regular tea," I said, "and let Ernie take care of things."

"He's busy right now. Did I tell you that the lake is up to the house?"

"Good grief, and it's supposed to rain later today." That's when I remembered a few nights ago when I'd thought I saw the moon reflected on the Quintana lawn. So I hadn't been hallucinating after all.

"I'll see you later," she murmured.

"Bye, Allie." I dropped the phone, grabbed a potholder and pulled the oven door open. The cookies looked fine until later when they cooled. Chipping them off the cookie sheet, I saw that their little bottoms were black. It was mid-afternoon, and my peanut butter was all gone so I scraped cookie bottoms with a knife and layered the cookies in a pretty tin.

David came to the front door. I let him in. He looked wonderful.

"Is there a fire?" he asked, looking around.

"All taken care of," I smiled as we walked to the kitchen. "What time is Harley coming?"

"Around seven, which probably means eight. He said they'll get burgers on the way down." David looked up at a bit of residual cookie smoke wafting around the ceiling light.

"Can Harley cook?" I asked.

"Boy, can my son cook, he loves to cook but he never has time. Between the insurance business, an active five year old and a few dates here and there." David shrugged. "They're staying through Monday so we'll have a chance to get some good food into them."

"Looks like you're dressed up and ready to go to the funeral," I said.

"You might want to wash that dough out of your hair." His finger pointed to the thick salt and pepper hair above his own forehead.

"I was heading for the shower when you knocked on the door. Next time you see me I'll look like a shiny new penny."

"Those things are pretty outdated," he laughed, as he sat down at the table and checked his cell phone for the latest sports news.

Once I was clean and dry, I hauled out my seldom used little black dress. The hem length might not have been up with the times, but it was my only black outfit dressy enough for an important funeral. Whenever Alicia hurt, I hurt—kind of like having a little sister to worry about. Black boots, a string of beads and some lipstick, and I was ready to go.

I grabbed the tin of cookies and followed David out to his Miata. The heavy rain had quit, but there was still a fine mist in the air that felt good on my flushed face.

Our trip to Santa Cruz was relatively quiet. My mind went through yesterday's encounter with the girls on horseback and the bracelet full of brilliant colored-glass jewels. I was never one to wear a lot of jewelry, but I wished I'd remembered to wear it to the funeral. Where was that bracelet anyway? Probably still in my pants pocket, the pair of Levis I threw into the laundry basket last night. I made a mental note to retrieve the bracelet before the pants were stuffed into the washing machine.

"You're pretty quiet today," David said, skillfully slipping his Miata into a parking space at the curb. His parallel parking technique had us nestled between Alicia's SUV and a green pickup truck. As we walked half a block to the Parthenon steps in cool semi-sunshine, I had a feeling I'd forgotten something.

I stopped walking and remembered the cookies.

David looked back at me.

"I need the key to your car. I forgot the cookies."

He handed me the key and I hurried back for the tin canister. As I passed the green truck, I noticed it had a Park Ranger seal of California on the door. "Those rangers really get around," I said to myself, as I hurried back to David with the cookies. We entered the building and I handed the tin to a greeter who looked at it like it was a box of Cracker Jacks from the dollar store. I explained to Lurch that they were cookies for the reception.

Alicia had said she wanted a small turnout and that's what it was. Her neighbors—a nice elderly couple—sat in the front row. The couple quietly welcomed us as we scooted around them along the front pew. I looked down the short row of people to Alicia, Ernie and Trigger. Alicia looked in control of her emotions, but Ernie had concern for her written all over his face.

Trigger busily shuffled through pamphlets and a song book, looking dapper in his navy blue suit and new haircut.

I casually turned my head to check out the twenty something empty pews behind us, spotting a ranger uniform in the back row. My quick glance registered a tall, heavy-set man in his thirties with reddish hair, ruddy complexion and eyes so blue I could see their color from twenty rows away.

In front of us was the tasteful casket Alicia had picked out, with a half a dozen white lilies laid across the top. It wasn't showy, but somehow it seemed just right for poor Maria. The priest said some kind words, probably used many times before, and ended the service with an invitation for refreshments in the reception hall.

I looked back twenty rows to see if the ranger would stay or go. He chose to stay and met up with our little group congregating in one corner of the great hall off the sanctuary. We had our choice of fresh coffee, iced tea or lemonade plus peanut butter cookies. I'd thought there would be other cookie choices. Suddenly my cookies had become very important. Alicia thanked me for bringing them.

Mr. Ranger stepped into our little circle holding a cookie in his large freckled hand. "Excuse me, are you Alicia Quintana?"

"Yes, I am," Alicia said, obviously surprised to see an outsider at the funeral.

"My name's Howard Winkle."

"Oh, yes, you…" Alicia choked.

"I'm so sorry for your loss," Howard blushed red. "I'm the one who found your sister."

My ears perked up big time. I looked up into the clear blue eyes of the six-foot-three park ranger. "Do you have any idea how this murder happened?"

David gave me a quick warning look, like "Drop it!"

"I'm sort of following up on this case," Howard said importantly. "I happen to know that the Sheriff's Department is pretty stretched right now, and I'd like to help you get some answers. Mrs. Quintana, your sister was a very pretty lady, and she was nice to me."

"Thank you," Alicia whispered.

"Let's step out to the hall," I suggested to Howard.

"Call me Howie," he said, as we moved to the doorway and out into the empty hallway. Several velvet-cushioned benches lined the walls of the long entry. A draft gave me the shivers, as I sat down next to the large redhead. My senses had been electrified by his statement to Alicia.

"Howie, is it true that you talked to Maria?"

"Yeah, she and this foreign guy were wanting to take the train up Bear Mountain. It was getting dark and cold and they weren't dressed for the cold. I told them they could buy jackets at the General store and then get their tickets right across the street."

"Is that what they did?"

"I think so because, like I said, I was the one who found her the next day and she was wearing one of our Roaring Camp jackets—the lady's version of course. I could tell she was a real lady." Howard's eyes looked moist. He looked away.

"Did you notice what she was wearing, her jewelry or anything else?"

"I don't remember jewelry, but I remember she was wearing these leather sandals…can you imagine sandals in cold weather?"

"Howard, who else was on that train? Anyone suspicious looking?"

Howard furrowed his brow. "I remember the gentleman Maria was with."

"That would have been her brother," I said. "Anyone else?"

"I remember a big guy with black spiky hair." Howie's voice drifted off.

"Because someone was chasing them," I said, "and I imagine that someone is after Maria's brother even as we speak. We don't know where the brother is now. Do you have any information that would help us?"

"Well, I remember he was wearing the same kind of leather sandals."

"Howard, do you have a card? I'm probably going to want to ask you more questions."

He handed me his card and laughed. "My whole reason for coming here today was to question the people who knew Maria."

"Well, the light turnout is because she didn't live around here. We think Maria and her brother came up from Mexico." I handed him one of my business cards.

"That makes sense, but why take the Halloween train ride? It's for fun and mostly for families." Howard stared at the marble floor. "So he was her brother."

"Do you have a family, Howie?"

"I had a wife and baby daughter...drunk driver. We'll be in touch," he said, as he stood up quickly and walked out of the building.

I stood up and watched Howard leave, a family type of man with no family. Finally I turned and walked back to the reception room where the Quintanas and their neighbors chatted. Alicia asked me if we could take Trigger home rather than have him go to the grave site. I told her we'd be happy to have some quality time with him.

When we arrived at the Quintana house, Trigger warned us to walk the plank or we'd have wet shoes. Sure enough, a twelve-foot long plank had been placed on top of the sidewalk slanting up to the second porch step which was close to being under water. We balanced our way along the foot-wide plank that felt like it was just about ready to float. All it needed was the smack of a champagne bottle for the send-off.

Trigger knew right where the hidden key was and proudly opened the door for us. We hung our jackets in the foyer above Ernie's big rubber boots, and settled ourselves on the couch. Trigger told us how his father had floated their canoe halfway around the house and right into the garage. He explained that their two neighbors' houses, also on the west end of the lake, were flooded. He and his dad hoped the rain would stop soon, but his mother wasn't paying much attention to the problem since the first and second floors weren't flooded.

David checked his phone and his watch periodically, worried that Harley and Monica might arrive in Aromas at any time.

"Don't worry, David, Roger will answer the door," I said.

"You're right. I don't know what I was worried about."

"Who's Roger?" Trigger asked.

I stood up and walked to one of the large windows facing the lake. "We don't really know who Roger is because he has amnesia."

"If he has am..neesha how do you know his name is Roger?"

David explained that was a temporary name given to him by my Aunt Clara.

"Where's your peddle boat, Trigger?" I asked.

"It floated away in the first big storm. Mom says we'll find it before Easter. I sure hope so," he sighed. "Did you know that we had a duck swimming in our garage?"

I checked my watch. It was seven and David's cell phone was ringing.

He answered. "Yeah, Harley, what time did you say? Nine? Okay, that'll be swell. See ya soon." He stuffed the phone back into his pocket.

Trigger put the *Seven O'clock News* on and we watched the weather gal tell us it wouldn't rain for the next three days. I couldn't help rolling my eyes, but I really wanted to believe Ms. Botox.

"David, what are your plans for tomorrow?" I asked, snuggling in beside him on the sofa.

"I don't have any…but now that I know it won't be raining, maybe we can go somewhere," he said. "Maybe I'll take Harley and Monica to Roaring Camp."

Trigger looked at David with big yearning eyes.

"Sorry, Trigger, you have school tomorrow," he said. "Monica will miss kindergarten, but it's okay because she's visiting her grandpa."

A sudden scream, a few groans and then laughter had us all looking in the direction of the front door.

Ernie looked around the corner into the living room, "I'll be back…just have to run a hot bath for Alicia. She fell off the plank."

Poor shivering Alicia moved past her husband, draped in dripping wet clothes, and stiffly climbed the stairs leading to the master bath and bedroom. Ernie raced up the stairs behind her.

It wasn't like Alicia to lose her balance.

I told Ernie we were leaving. David was anxious to be home for Harley, and I had prep-work to do for my mural job. I needed to load my paints and equipment into the truck and check off a long list of things not to forget. Hopefully I'd remember where I put the list.

CHAPTER 8

Monday morning my alarm clock jolted me out of my lackadaisical vacation mode and into the real world of commuter traffic and work. I was thankful for work, but they didn't call it "work" for nothing. After sixty-eight minutes of stop and go traffic I finally reached my destination, the Felton Recreation Center. One year ago, the town of Felton became the beneficiary of a sixty-year-old church. It had been built like an oversized barn with a proportionately small steeple on top. It sat on two acres of flat land just two blocks west of Felton and two blocks east of the deer crossing sign where I'd recently found Roger lying in the mud.

The original seventies church building had flooded last year so the doors were closed for a six-month repair job. When the church was finally ship-shape, the parishioners had already found churches they liked and never came back to the patched up building. Those in charge sent their Reverend Hammer to a church in Arizona and donated the property to the town of Felton.

I parked as close to the Center's front entrance as I could and unloaded two ladders. Then came two large canvas bags full of support items such as masking tape, Goof-off, alcohol, chalk, a snap-line, sketches, empty plastic containers, rags, pallets, brushes, camera, a thermos of hot tea and a sack lunch. My last trip to the truck was for last minute items such as a three-foot level, a warmer jacket, knitted cap, scarf, leg warmers, and an extra sweater in case the building didn't have heat. As a muralist, I never knew ahead of time what to expect so I always imagined the worst and prepared for it.

Unfortunately, I was right about a lack of heat. The two exterior doors were open to the elements—in this case, frost. Of course, the young men working in the church building didn't feel the cold, but as a mature woman I quickly turned into a hormonal popsicle. As soon as I could, I sat on the hardwood floor and pulled on my leggings and knitted cap. I tried to picture a hot summer day in my mind but my mind knew a lie when it heard one.

"Josephine," a crusty voice behind me said, "looks like you're ready to paint."

I jumped up. "Doug, good morning. Yes, I'll be painting as soon as I arrange all this equipment. My painters won't be here until tomorrow. One had a death in the family and the other has classes on Mondays and Wednesdays."

"Let me know if you need help with anything," he offered, and walked away.

I wondered where he was when I'd lugged everything into the building.

One of the young workers wearing white coveralls walked up and asked me if I'd seen his earbuds.

"Sorry, I just got here; name's Josephine."

"I'm Chris; call me if you need anything," he said.

"Chris, I just want to thank you for following my instructions. The wall is just right—blue on the top and green on the bottom."

He smiled and moved quickly away, like a painter who follows directions and doesn't question the peculiar blue and green motif. A few smears of green paint decorated his white overalls. My paint clothes were more colorful than his. I didn't wear a uniform or overalls; I just wore my old clothes that were ready for Goodwill. Once they were covered in paint splotches, they usually held together for several more years. Even my shoes were colorfully spattered.

Once my equipment was organized and piled against a side wall, I began drawing the basic mural design on the fourteen-foot high by thirty-foot long wall using a stick of white chalk and a level. The steam engine took a lot of time, whereas the 1880's type buildings were easy to draw once the proper perspective was established. I had plenty of ghost town pictures to draw from, plus actual photos of Roaring Camp. I even had pictures from a magazine that featured the camp's annual Civil War Reenactment. Unfortunately, the photo was black and white. I'd have to research the exact colors of the uniforms.

When I finally decided to take a lunch break, I looked up and there was Alicia. She wore one of her usual paint outfits, minus the paint, since she hardly ever spilled or smeared anything.

"Am I in time to take you to lunch?" she asked.

Suddenly I lost interest in my sack lunch. "That would be great, Allie. Where do you want to go?"

"I thought we could grab a burger over at Roaring Camp."

"Allie, you're kidding, right?"

"No, I'm interested in finding out exactly what happened to my sis..." her voice dropped down to a whisper.

"Maybe we can solve this thing together," I said, thinking how strange it was to have my friend join in the search for justice. Suddenly I felt free to share information and ask for help. I'd been liberated from putting up the usual secrecy barriers surrounding murder mysteries. If only I could get Mom and David to accept my inquisitive nature.

We piled into Alicia's Volvo SUV and five minutes later entered Cowell State Park. We parked near the museum and walked a wide paved path up to the railroad tracks that ran through the western town. It was twelve fifteen and the train was in position to start its once-a-day trip up Bear Mountain.

"Allie, we might be able to go on the ride if we hurry."

"We probably should," she said, following me to the other side of the train station building where the tickets were sold. Not a single soul stood in line for a ticket. Alicia tapped on the window and a woman opened it.

"Two tickets please, she said, handing over her credit card.

A loud letting go of steam startled me. Then the whistle blew twice.

Water dripped from dozens of copper tubes coiled over the engine.

I watched the cowboy-sheriff ride his horse around the old engine and six open-air wooden cars. The passengers, mostly families and groups of school children, cheered and waved to the man on horseback.

The woman in the window handed Alicia two tickets and motioned for us to hurry and get a seat, which we did. We had a choice of seats since the benches were less than full. After all, it was a weekday and almost winter. I chose the third car and Alicia climbed aboard right behind me.

Just as we sat down, the train lurched, then ground its way up to slow-train speed. The locomotive kept that same speed all the way through the forest and up the steeper grades, eventually stopping near the top of the mountain. We watched the conductor, who'd already gathered tickets and talked a blue streak into a portable mic, suddenly jump off the train. He took a few steps over to a large lever sticking up from a set of side tracks and pushed it into a different position. The young conductor then climbed aboard and continued his dialogue into the mic.

Dixiana, engine number one, began moving slowly up hill. We made a very long left loop and after a short stop, we headed back downhill. Soon we were riding on the same original tracks we'd started out on.

As the mighty train chugged down the mountain and over the trestle, we looked down about thirty feet to the rocky area I'd already explored. I saw the yellow tape around the rock where Maria had landed.

"Oh look, Jo, a little tree…it's kind of whitish. Isn't that odd?"

"It's an albino redwood," I said, as if I knew all about such things.

"How did you know that?"

"I was here yesterday looking for clues. A couple of teenage girls on horseback were in love with Solow and answered some of my questions. One of them named Grace gave me a bracelet that she'd found near that little albino tree. I think it's pretty, but too glitzy for my taste. I think it would look great on you, Allie, not that you're the glitzy type, but with your dark hair you look good in jewel tones."

"I'd like to see it," she said, matter of factly.

"It's at home in my pants pocket."

"Don't you think it's coincidental that the bracelet was found near where they found Maria?" Alicia cocked her head.

"How did you know that was the area?"

"I saw the yellow tape..." she lowered her gaze to the wooden floor.

Most of the people around us were busy filming and snapping pictures with their phones. Many of them were pointing straight up to the sky at the tops of old growth redwoods towering above us, preserved by Mr. Isaac Graham and later by the state of California. Graham had set up the first sawmill west of the Mississippi on the acres that eventually became Roaring Camp. Twenty-five years later, it was the first virgin stand of coastal redwoods to be protected by the State of California from logging. Thankfully, the two-thousand-year-old trees are still there, admired by thousands of tourists from all over the world.

Our car rocked and clattered as the antique locomotive made a long oval, straightened and slowed, letting off huge bursts of steam. The whistle blew several times as we made a grand entrance into town. Our seven mile trip was over and so was our lunch hour.

I stood up, stretched and climbed out of the car. Alicia was right behind me.

Out of the corner of my eye, I saw a child running toward us from a couple cars away. She yelled something which I ignored.

Alicia turned around. "Jo, it's Monica!"

I turned around. "What? Oh my gosh; it is." I bent down, stretched my arms out and let Monica run right into them. David and Harley were right behind her.

"Hi there, Harley," I said. He raised a thumb and smiled.

"I thought you had to work today," David said.

Alicia stepped up and explained, "This is our lunch break."

David nodded his head. "Working for yourself has a few benefits." He smiled and hugged me. "How'd you like the ride?"

"Terrific! But our lunch hour is up, and then some," I sighed.

"We're going over to the blacksmith shop," Harley said.

"Sorry, we have to go back to work. Have fun." As a self-employed muralist and employer, I'd set up strict rules years ago for myself and my employees.

Alicia and I hurried back to the Felton Rec Center. She parked the car and we hustled inside. My friend began organizing the paint equipment while I finished drawing the rough placement of the Roaring Camp mural.

"Jo, are there any other facts or clues you haven't told me about?"

"There's one thing. Remember I told you about seeing a green ranger's pickup truck? It was parked near your house, my house and the grocery store and then there it was—parked in front of the mortuary. Well, I talked to the driver of the truck..."

"That would be Howie," she smiled.

"Yeah, anyway, he said he witnessed your brother and sister getting on the train. He thought Maria was quite beautiful and a real lady."

"Thank you, Jo. That's sweet...but why's he following you?"

"He's trying to figure this thing out just like we are. I think Howard's doing it because he was really taken by your sister." I handed Alicia half of my peanut butter and sliced pear sandwich.

"Thanks, Jo, I was getting hungry." She took a bite. "Maybe we should combine forces with Howie."

"Yeah, but just long enough to find out everything he knows," I said as I washed a bite of sandwich down with cold tea.

"You don't trust him?"

"Not completely. Now tell me about the flooding around your house."

"Oh, Jo, it'll go down as soon as it stops raining." Obviously she couldn't be bothered.

"Is something blocked up? Why doesn't the lake drain?" I asked.

"Okay, water comes into the lake from the eastern mountains, but it evaporates over the summer. There's no river, no outlet, no other way for the water to get to the Pajaro River. This winter happens to be wetter than most, and the lake stayed pretty full all last summer. But Ernie and our two neighbors have been offered the loan of a pump from the county. All we have to do is keep it filled with gasoline. My understanding is that the water will be pumped through hoses stretched across College Avenue so it can flow into the Pajaro River."

"Sounds like a major project."

"They estimate it will take at least four weeks of constant pumping to bring the water level down a few inches. The three flooded households will share the expense. In the meantime, Ernie's building a better ramp to the front door."

At three thirty, Alicia and I stood back and evaluated what I'd drawn on the wall. She pointed out a couple of things that needed to be changed. One obvious thing was the Civil War Reenactment. For being in the background, the figures were too big. They were almost as big as the people lined up at the station and mingling around town. I wasn't worried because it was only a preliminary placement sketch—kind of a practice run.

"I like the idea of the three horses in the foreground," Alicia said. "Are those the girls you met?"

I nodded, "Yep, won't they be surprised. The third person is the sheriff. But there won't be a lot of detail in the faces, just hair color and hats, boots…and, of course, the coloring of the horses. Would you like to paint a few clouds?"

"Sure, I'll get started." She deftly prepared a pallet in various shades of white, spread the legs of my eight foot ladder, climbed it and began brushing in wispy clouds. Some of the clouds went all the way up to the fourteen foot ceiling.

Two weeks ago my instructions to the contractor had assured us minimal time on the old eight foot ladder. The painters had painted a swath of light blue paint across the top five feet of the thirty-foot long wall. All we had to do was add a few clouds. Low hills and Bear Mountain would cover some of that blue sky, creating a backdrop for the old western town.

As I corrected the proportions of my reenactment armies, I felt eyes on my back. When I turned my head, I saw someone watching us from the main entrance. He was easy to recognize in his all ranger-green uniform and reddish hair. I put my chalk down and walked over to the door.

"Hey, Howie, how's it goin?"

"I have some new information."

Instantly my heart rate sped up. "I'm listening."

"I've been going through video that came from a camera in the rafters above the ticket window."

"The ticket window at the train station?"

"Yep, hardly anyone knows it's there. I had to get special permission from my boss to look at the tapes."

"Find anything with Maria in it?"

"No, but I did see the guy who was with her buying tickets, and minutes later, I recognized another guy…the one I saw seated on the train next to Maria."

"Did you ride the train that night?" I asked.

"Not exactly…at the last minute I got on the train looking for Dan, the conductor. I had a text from my boss. She said to watch for vandals. I wasn't sure what that meant, but I wanted to mention it to Dan before the train left the station."

"So you climbed onto the train…" I prompted Howard.

"Yeah, and I happened to see the handsome couple sitting in the last car at the end of the bench. As I stood there, a big guy with black hair and a scar on his cheek sat down on the other side of the woman. She looked scared."

"So what did you do?"

"Right then the train started to move forward. There was lots of steam, people chatting and the train whistle blew so I couldn't hear what anybody said. And I never got my message to Dan because I had to get off the train quickly or go for the whole ride. I thought I couldn't spare the time," Howard said. "I should have stayed." He looked down at the floor. "I should have helped her."

"Howard, you had no way of knowing something bad was about to happen. Don't blame yourself."

"The thing is, I see hundreds of tourists at the park every day. This big guy wasn't the usual tourist enjoying the scenery. And the way he was dressed…white shirt, light jacket, slacks and leather sandals! He wasn't from around here, unless he owns the Mexican restaurant in Felton. But I know he doesn't," Howard corrected himself. "He seemed to know the couple…and she was afraid of him. I saw it in her eyes."

CHAPTER 9

Tuesday morning I woke up feeling excited about the Felton mural. Alicia had painted lovely cloud configurations the day before, getting us off to a good start. I looked forward to seeing my other painter, Kyle Larson, who attended the local university in Santa Cruz and worked for me whenever he could fit it into his schedule——in this case, Tuesdays and Fridays.

Leaving Solow at home, I drove to Watsonville's Lake District and parked in front of Alicia's house, now up to its gills in murky green lake water. I tooted the horn and a minute later, watched Alicia walk the plank, her purse in one hand and her lunch box in the other. She laughed with relief as she climbed into the passenger seat.

"Guess I'm a little nervous ever since I fell off the ramp."

"I would be too. Is that the pump you told me about?" I pointed to a large yellow engine with several fat hoses attached and positioned across College Avenue, probably all the way to the Pajaro River.

Alicia nodded. "That's the monster we named Clangor."

"Sure makes a lot of noise."

"You should hear it at night," she said, her eyes rimmed in red, "and poor Ernie has to get up at one o'clock every morning to pour gas into the monster. Our neighbors are retired, so they handle the dayshift."

"I hope you're getting enough sleep."

"Don't worry, Jo, we'll get used to the noise. Trigger sleeps right through it, even when Clangor backfires."

Tuesday's traffic turned out to be less than Monday's, allowing us to begin work right on time at nine o'clock. Doug looked up from sanding the countertop in the far corner of the room. I wanted to explain to him that my morning was not simple and that a nine o'clock arrival was a realistic goal.

My day began with Solow not coming home after his Fluffy chase. I found him at David's house. David asked if I'd taste test his new recipe for buttermilk pancakes. I accidentally spilled syrup on my shirt and had to go home and change. Then I drove to Watsonville, picked up Alicia and commuted thirty more miles to Felton.

Doug probably woke up, scratched his belly, pulled on the pants he wore all week and drove five blocks to the Center. He'd worked on the curved countertop all day Monday and now he was about to apply a last coat of varnish. That corner of the room had been designed to look like a malt shop for the kids. What kid would even know what a malt was? Oh, well, it was a cute colorful place for kids to spend time.

"Jo, are we painting the foothills and Bear Mountain today?" Alicia asked.

"Yep, and here comes Kyle just in time to help."

Kyle shed his motorcycle helmet and leather jacket, exposing his latest piercings and a bit of tattoo showing at the end of his sleeve.

"Nice clouds, Alicia," he said.

"Thanks." She gave him a sweet smile.

"Good to see you, Kyle," I said. "See if you can find us another ladder. A six-footer would be good." He turned and walked across the room to Doug at the "soda fountain," who sent him to another room that used to be the kitchen and fellowship hall combined.

Minutes later, Kyle was back with a six-foot ladder.

Alicia excused herself and entered the kitchen area. From there she would find an all-gender bathroom. While she was gone, Kyle and I discussed colors of paint for the hills and meadow. We loaded our pallets and climbed our ladders. He was assigned the middle ten foot section, I took Bear Mountain on the right and Alicia would have the left ten feet.

Many of our landscape paintings had involved some kind of uneven terrain as a background such as hills or mountains, with interesting subjects in the middle ground and larger (up-close) subjects down low in the foreground. It was all about creating depth and we were the magicians assigned to the task.

Alicia finally came back to claim a pallet and three of her favorite brushes. She set up her ladder, checked the sketch taped to the wall and began painting her ten-foot section of hills with a two inch brush. She began by connecting her hill with Kyle's, working from right to left to make it one long mountain range. They had similar styles and used the same three greens, a couple of browns, plus blue and purple for shadowing. Later, subtle yellow washes would turn it into a sunny day.

After an intense hour of painting, Alicia climbed down from her ladder and walked over to the kitchen. Ten minutes later, she was back on the ladder working on a patch of lupin. A couple of splotches of blue paint stuck to her black t-shirt.

A little after twelve, I suggested we break for lunch, as I dropped my brush into the water bucket. I walked over to the kitchen and multi-use room and beyond to the one functional, remodeled restroom. I opened the door and was bombarded with lingering cigarette smoke. I swung the door back and forth many times trying to swish the smell out.

When I returned to my friends, I complained, "Someone was smoking in the restroom. Can you believe it?"

Kyle's jaw dropped. "Like, someone is smoking, not vaping?"

"Yep, it's a wild world out there." I laughed.

By noon we'd each laid out a rough set of hills. Shading, highlights and details would follow. I stood back about fifteen feet squinting at the wall and sizing it up.

"You guys taking a lunch break?" Doug asked.

I nodded.

"Best place if ya like Mexican food is the Taqueria over at the corner of Highway Nine and Graham Hill Road."

"Actually, Alicia and I brought our lunches today. I'm not sure about Kyle."

"They have a great outdoor patio where you can eat, if you don't mind birds and dogs," Doug continued, his sour breath too near for comfort.

I stepped away and squinted at the mural one more time.

"We'll probably try it out tomorrow. Thanks for the recommendation," I said.

Alicia walked up to me and asked if we could eat our lunch at Roaring Camp. She was beginning to sound like me once I was on the trail of a murder suspect.

Kyle joined us as we stared at the mural, and said he'd be eating at the Taqueria.

Alicia and I drove less than a mile to Roaring Camp. This time I parked the truck in the upper parking area and walked across a covered bridge leading straight into the park. We were sitting on a bench in the cool sunlight eating our sandwiches when a familiar looking woman wearing a long dress, obviously designed for "Little House On The Prairie" characters, smiled at us and stopped to talk.

"I remember you. You sold me a map," I said.

"Map of Bear Mountain," she added.

"That's the one."

Her eyes were fixed on Alicia who was chewing a bite of her roast beef sandwich. "And you look familiar," the woman said. "Don't I know you from somewhere?"

Alicia looked up. "I'm sorry. I don't believe we've met."

"Oh, now I remember. It wasn't you; it was another pretty lady, but you remind me of her."

Bells and whistles went off in my head as electricity surged through my body. I remembered a week ago when I saw Maria's picture on the TV screen and later in the newspaper, and the strong feeling I'd had that she looked familiar. There was no denying the similarities.

The woman plopped down next to Alicia. "My name's Dolly Winkle. I work across the street at the General Store."

I leaned forward and turned to Dolly. "By any chance, did you see Maria, the lady who fell out of the train?"

She closed her eyes for a moment. "They say she was murdered," Dolly stammered. "Yes, I saw her in the store and in the newspaper. She sure looked a lot like you, miss," Dolly said to Alicia. "Nice lady…she asked me to wear her ring until she got back."

Tears gathered in Alicia's eyes. "We are…were…sisters."

"Oh dear, I'm so sorry. I never told this to anybody, but I could tell that your sister was scared of something or someone." Dolly began pulling on her pinky finger. Finally, the ring popped off. "Here, this was Maria's." She dropped the ring into Alicia's hand.

Alicia looked stunned. She stared at the pink stone encased in gold filigree as Dolly stood up, said goodbye and walked briskly away. Her big bonnet rested on sloped shoulders as her skirt ruffled in the breeze.

"Jo, do you think it's real?"

"I'm no jeweler, but I think it is since the other ring was real. Looks like another three or four carats to me. Put it on your finger so you don't lose it."

Alicia slipped the ring onto her right-hand ring finger.

"It fits," she said, holding her trembling hand out for me to see. "I'll put it in my purse. It's much too flashy for my taste." She hugged her purse all the way to my truck. Once we were on our way back to the Rec Center she relaxed a bit.

"By the way, here's the bracelet Grace gave me." I pulled it out of my pocket and handed it to Alicia. Her eyes were wide as her jaw dropped.

"Are you feeling okay?" I asked.

"Jo, that's the third time today you asked that question. I know you want to keep me from being sad, but I'm fine. I just need to think about my sister and feel sad. I think that's normal." She dropped the bracelet into her purse.

"So why are your hands shaking?"

"A little, maybe…I'm cold. Don't worry, Jo, I'll be fine."

Once we started another round of painting, my mind was into the work—mostly. In the far corner of the room, Doug watched his lacquer dry while Wildbrush Mural painters created hills, mountains, a meadow and a trestle. By design, Alicia painted the left end of the wall while Kyle added the trestle in the middle section. Maybe it was silly, but I didn't want her to paint the train trestle and be reminded of what had happened there on Halloween night.

At mid-afternoon, I decided I needed to stretch my legs with a little walkabout. Alicia left her ladder perch, grabbed her purse and followed me out the front door into fading sunshine. We sat on a bench watching Highway Nine traffic slowly, painfully work its way toward Ben Lomond and Boulder Creek. San Lorenzo Valley High School had just let out and there were all kinds of interesting kids' cars on display.

"Allie, what are you doing?"

"This is called a cigarette, and I'm going to smoke it," she said, as one shaky hand tried to light the tip. "Can you help me?" She handed me a lighter.

"Help you smoke? Are you crazy? What kind of an example is that for the teenagers?"

"Never mind; I can do it." Tears streamed down her face as she fumbled with the lighter.

"Oh, Allie, I'm so stupid. You need to do this, don't you?" I took the lighter and lit her cigarette. She took two long puffs and then squashed the butt with her foot.

"Ouch!" She whispered to herself.

"Didn't you tell me your foot hurts when the weather's damp?"

Alicia chuckled, "It's my rainy day friend. Did I ever tell you how it got that way?"

"No, just that it goes way back to when you were a little girl."

Alicia took a deep breath and coughed. She looked at me and said, "Don't worry; I don't plan to smoke much longer. I just have to get through this…you know? Anyway, when I was six years old my sister, Maria, and I were doing what we did every day. We had our paper bags full of gum packets, and we ran up to cars as they came to a stop at an intersection near the hospital."

"Did you have to walk a long way to get there?" I asked.

"It didn't seem long because we talked and laughed a lot on the way. One day, I ran up to a big black car thinking, "These people are rich and will buy lots of gum." Actually, we thought that about all the nicer cars. Sometimes people would buy from us, and every peso went to Mama so we could have food to eat. I was so excited when I saw the big black car with a pretty lady in the passenger seat, that I wasn't careful and I got too close. The back tire ran over my foot.

"What did you do?"

"I screamed, of course. I remember trying so hard not to cry, but I couldn't stop."

"You were only six. Of course, you'd cry," I said.

"I can still see that lady dressed in blue, looking like a lovely angel. She opened her door and scooped me up into her arms. Her husband examined my dirty bare foot as I bawled my eyes out. I felt so ashamed for crying and ashamed for not having shoes. I remember his gentle touch. He told his wife that my foot needed to be x-rayed. I was horrified. People who went to the hospital never came out, at least in my world. My real father never came out of the hospital except to be buried. We kids never knew what he died of."

"How old were you when your father died?" I asked.

"Young enough that I had no idea what was going on. The only thing I remember was being left over night with my grandparents. I was about four years old and remember wanting to go home."

"So how did you end up with the new parents?"

"It turned out that the black car had been on its way to the hospital because the nice American man was a doctor. He and his wife came across the border a couple times a year to do volunteer work at our local hospital—a very poor facility. Papa drove us to the hospital. I called him 'Papa' until I graduated from college," Alicia laughed. "Anyway, I had broken bones in my foot and he put a cast on it. I stayed a couple of nights at the hospital and my future adoptive parents were with me much of the time, along with my oldest brother, Del."

"How old was Del at the time?"

"He was about twelve years old. He worked at the bank sweeping floors and running errands. My mother was so proud of him. We all were. I realize now that he was the one who provided the most for our family. He had become a father figure for Maria and me."

"So what about your new parents?"

"Well, they struck some kind of deal with my mother. Actually, they supported my family for many years. I wasn't against going with the Americans. I liked wearing pretty shoes and I loved my new Papa and Mama. Not a hard pill to swallow," she smiled.

"I'm surprised you weren't in contact with your family. Surely your new mom and dad could have…"

"No, that was part of the arrangement. It was to be like most adoptions in those days—no contact with the old family. To this day, I don't even know my real last name. My adoptive papa continued to volunteer at the hospital twice a year until he was too old to drive down there. My new mom never went to Tijuana again. Before she died, she told me that Papa always checked up on my family and saw to their needs while he was there."

I heard footsteps behind us and turned my head.

"Kyle, how's it going?"

"Like, I painted some redwoods, but I need you to see if it's what you want. I thought you two walked to Ben Lomond or something."

"No, just sitting here talking," I said.

"Some ranger dude was looking for you."

I rolled my eyes; the guy was everywhere. "So what did he want?"

"He just asked me to give you his card." Kyle handed me a green card with smudges of brown and purple paint on it.

"Sorry," he laughed, as he inspected the paint on his fingertips.

I turned the card over in my hand. "What's this?"

"I don't know who D. W. is. Try the number and see," he suggested.

Pushing the card into my Levi pocket, I asked Kyle if the ranger dude had any news about the murder.

"He wants you to call him," Kyle grinned. "Said he wants to arrange a meeting." He raised his eyebrows a few times and laughed.

CHAPTER 10

Wednesday morning arrived via a fog bank that eventually engulfed my little house and all of Aromas. It was as welcome as a shroud on a sunbather. Smothered in dim light, I prepared myself for another day of painting. My shower was hot, my breakfast hot and my goodbyes to Solow were reluctant. I finally drove away, unable to see more than ten feet in front of the truck. Aromas residents never knew when a pocket of fog would settle on the town. It was an inconvenience that cleared up once Alicia and I were a few miles north of Santa Cruz.

"Jo, Trigger mentioned a man named Roger. How do you know him?"

"He's a guy with amnesia who's staying with David for a while."

"How does he know his name is Roger?"

"He doesn't. Clara named him Roger and it just stuck."

Alicia nodded her head and changed the subject.

"Did you call Howard about that D. W. on the back of his business card?" she asked.

I squirmed in my seat. "Not yet; David came over last night and we had a lovely evening. I was so tired I just wanted to enjoy my guy," I said, still enjoying memories from our precious time together.

Alicia looked at me like I was wasting time. Every minute counted in finding Maria's murderer. Why wasn't I on it twenty-four-seven?

I drove with one hand, pulled Howard's card out of my purse with the other and handed the card to Alicia. She took the hint, pulled out her phone and rang up the number on the back.

A woman who sounded like Dolly answered her phone after several rings.

"Sorry, whoever this is," she said, "call me back later. I'm driving."

Alicia looked at me, "She's like you, no Bluetooth."

Just then, a cute little black and white Mini Cooper whizzed by us in the fast lane. The driver wore a blue bonnet.

"Did you see that?" I stammered. "That's Dolly; she must be late for work."

"If we had a set time to be at work, we'd be considered late too," Alicia laughed. "But why's Dolly coming from Santa Cruz?"

I smiled. Ironically, Alicia saw mystery in everyone and everything lately.

After driving the steep curvy Graham Hill Road down to Felton, I made a left at the four-way intersection and cruised to the end of town. The Rec Center parking lot hosted three regular workman-type pickups plus Howard's ranger truck. The man was everywhere it seemed, until we entered the building.

Looking up from a second round of sanding of the counter top, Doug cut the power and the whole place went silent. No radios or pods spewing out what was considered to be music in those days.

"Your ranger friend was here a minute ago," Doug said.

"Yeah, we saw his truck. I wonder where he went." I looked at Alicia. "Maybe we need to call Dolly and find out why he gave us her number."

The old Alicia would have rolled her eyes and accused me of being a snoop, but the new Alicia was on board. She wanted to know anything and everything—to the point that it was driving me a little bit nuts.

"Did I tell you the ranger had a black eye?" Doug said.

"Oh dear," Alicia groaned.

"Wonder how he got it," I said, thinking out loud.

"Yeah, well, he looked pathetic…like he'd been dragged through the briar patch." Doug scratched his balding head. "There must be a woman involved."

The silence was deafening.

Finally, Doug turned on the sander and went back to work.

We stepped back outside.

"Okay, Jo, I'm calling Dolly." She put the phone to her ear.

"This is Dolly…speaking."

I leaned in closer, not wanting to miss a word.

"Hi, Dolly, this is Alicia."

"Yes, my dear," (heavy breathing) "don't mind me, I'm running across the lot… to the main entrance. I'm late," she laughed. "Did you have a chance to talk to Howie?"

"No, that's why I'm calling. "

"He wanted to tell you…"

"Oh great, Now Dolly's phone's cut out. I'll try again later." Alicia slipped her phone into her pocket.

"Or we can go to Roaring Camp to eat our lunch," I suggested.

"That would be okay," Alicia said, "but I don't want to go back to the boulders and the trestle. I had a terrible nightmare last night."

"We'll just sit on a bench and eat our lunch and then visit the General Store," I promised.

Lunch on the bench went well. Nice and quiet until Dixiana pulled into the station, belching gobs of steam and blowing her whistle. A rush of fourth graders and teachers tramped by us and noisily claimed their seats on the train.

Ms. Dolly ran across the street, bonnet flapping, waving a handful of dollar bills. Breathless, she approached one of the teachers explaining that one of the little rug-rats had run off without his change. We watched as she handed over the bills and hustled back to the store.

"Jo, do you want the other half of my sandwich?"

"You need it more than I do. Are you losing weight?"

"Maybe a little. I'm just not as hungry as I used to be."

"Eat the rest of your sandwich later this afternoon," I advised, not wishing to wear her roast beef sandwich on my hips.

The cowboy sheriff waved his arms as his white horse pranced and danced,. The man herded people off the tracks right up to the moment when the train began to move forward. The whistle blew. One whole car, the one directly in front of us, was filled with students and teachers waving goodbye because that's what people do when they ride a train. We waved back because it's a natural reflex to return waves and smiles.

Once the train left the station, we walked across the tracks and ended up at the General Store. Dolly sat behind the counter with her feet resting on the counter top. She saw us, quickly put her feet down, stood up and adjusted her bonnet.

"Good morning, excuse me, good afternoon ladies," Dolly giggled.

"You look like you're having a good day," Alicia smiled.

"Yes, a day like all the other days..." Suddenly Dolly covered her face with her hands. "Sorry," she said, as her shoulders heaved.

Alicia was already beside her, one arm around her back. "Take it easy, Dolly. Have a seat," she said.

Dolly crumpled into her chair, still covering her face.

We stood there looking at each other, uncertain about what to do for her.

Finally, Dolly pulled herself together and looked up at us with teary eyes. "Please excuse me. I had a run-in with my boss today. I only have to work one more year until I can collect my social security. If I lose my job..."

"Why would you lose your job?" I asked. "You're very good with customers."

Dolly grabbed a tissue and blew her nose. "Early this morning, Howie and I had to go to Santa Cruz to look at a line-up, you know, at the police station. I was so nervous. We had to take turns looking at six men and point out the one who was seen on the train with

Maria and her gentleman friend. Howie and I both knew immediately that it was the muscular man with the scar on his cheek."

"How did you know that was the one?" I asked.

Dolly stared at her hands. "Because I saw the tape."

"And why were you privy to seeing the tape?" Alicia continued.

"Because Howie played the tape for me before it was handed over to the police. As soon as I saw the tape I recognized the big blocky man standing at the ticket window. It was the same man who was in the store while Maria was here buying herself a warm jacket. He lurked around the book room and kept an eye on her and the gentleman through the doorway." Dolly's cheeks flushed.

"Did Howard get in trouble for having the tape?" I asked.

Not yet." A couple of tears ran down her cheek. She blew her nose.

"Do the police know that you saw the tape?" Alicia asked.

Dolly shook her head. "The tape belongs to Roaring Camp Company."

"And you're under pressure to tell on Howard?" I handed her a tissue.

She looked up at me and nodded her head. "It took him a long time and a lot of work to finish school and get where he is today. I can't tell on him, he's my son," she whimpered.

"What does this have to do with possibly losing your job," I asked.

"Howie sort of found the park's surveillance tape and looked at it without permission. Then he shared it with me. I lied to my boss and said I didn't know anything about it. Now I wish I hadn't lied. I just didn't want to be fired," she sniffed.

"Let's hope it doesn't go that far," Alicia said. "Who has the tape now?"

"The Santa Cruz Police Department has it. They got it from Roaring Camp because Howie had already put it back where he found it."

"Then how does anyone know that you and Howie saw the tape?" I asked.

Dolly looked up at the rafters for a moment. "I was standing at the ticket window while Howie stood on a ladder putting the tape back in the machine. Apparently, it taped me. Of course, this was happening an hour before the park officially opened."

"What did your boss say when he found out?" Alicia asked.

Dolly wiped her forehead with a tissue. "My boss threatened to fire me. But the police like me," she smiled. "They said I was a big help with the line-up."

"Sounds to me like you were doing your civic duty," I said.

Alicia ran her hands over one of the jackets on the rack where Maria had probably put her hands while looking for something warm to wear.

"What can we do to help you, Dolly?" I asked. "We could put in a good word with your boss."

The poor woman sniffed and began organizing the coins, flags, tin sheriff's badges and little bags of peanuts on her counter, leaving just enough open space for sales transactions.

"Thank you, dear, but don't worry about me," Dolly said, "I'm a survivor."

"Dolly," Alicia said, "you have Josephine's card. Call her if you need any help. We don't want you to be fired."

"That's right," I nodded. "By the way, what happened to the man you picked out of the line-up?"

"The police called me an hour ago to tell me that they had to let him go. He posted bail."

"At least, they warned you he was out," I said.

Dolly picked up a feather duster and began her dusting routine.

I coughed a couple coughs and stepped away.

Alicia stepped back and looked around. "Did Maria buy a jacket like this one?"

Dolly stopped dusting mid-swipe. "That's the one, actually, we only carry that one style of jacket—the one with the train picture on the back. Works well for men and women and we have sizes all the way down to size four, for the little tykes. Notice the removable fuzzy vest inside the rainproof outer jacket." She looked like she was "in her groove" as she gave us her jacket spiel.

I asked Dolly about the bike helmets and rubber boots decorated in train motifs.

Alicia elbowed me and whispered, "Don't push it."

"Allie, wouldn't Trigger look cute in this train engineer hat?"

"He's a pretty mature ten-year-old."

"You're right, Allie. What size jacket does he wear?"

"I can take the hint," she said, pulling a boy's medium from the rack. She paid for the jacket and we said goodbye to Dolly.

As we headed back to the Rec Center, Alicia refolded the train jacket and smoothed it down across her lap.

I signaled to turn into the parking lot.

"I'm sorry, Jo, I didn't mean to…oh my! There's something in this pocket."

My truck tire bumped over the curb as I turned my head to look.

Alicia pulled out a lovely old-fashioned watch.

My side mirror scraped across the telephone pole at the entrance to the Rec parking lot. I pulled in beside a green ranger pickup and cut the engine.

"This looks like something from a hundred years ago," Alicia swooned.

"See what a good deal you got buying that jacket," I laughed.

"Jo, that's not funny. Someone's missing their watch."

Still sitting in the cab, I said, "I'm just wondering why all this jewelry is turning up. First the ring, then the bracelet and now an expensive looking watch. I wonder if it all belonged to Maria. If you were running away from home, wouldn't you take your valuables with you? Let's stop at the jewelers on the way home. We'll leave a little early, that is, if you have the ring and bracelet with you."

"They're in my purse. I'd planned to turn them over to lost and found at the park, but now it looks like they might have all belonged to my sister."

"I think you're right, Allie. It looks to me like she was trying to hide the watch from someone. We should go back tomorrow and ask Dolly to look around for more jewelry."

"Remember when Dolly told us that someone was lurking around the store, following Maria?" Alicia said, stepping out of her usual, 'I'll believe it when I see it,' character.

"Yep, and that might be why she looked frightened and hid the watch," I said. Finally, when we'd talked it out and decided the jewelry came from Maria, we climbed out of our seats and entered the building.

Doug looked up from the sink he was installing behind the soda counter. "You girls sure have it made," he teased. "How was lunch?"

"Sandwiches from home." I said, as if it were any of his business. I'd won the bid on the mural job. It was up to me to finish the job on time. How I did that was none of Doug's business. My official boss was a group of six Feltoners, the folks who'd generated enough donations to pay for a Recreation Center for the local kids.

Alicia and I took up painting where we left off, working for three hours straight. Apparently, Alicia was over her nicotine addiction. She hadn't taken a break in three hours, but I did. The restroom door was locked. I waited a few minutes, then knocked politely. Nothing. I asked if anyone was there. No one answered. I pounded on the door with my fist and finally went back to our painting.

"Jo, how can you paint with your legs crossed like that?" Alicia laughed.

"It's not easy. I'll try the restroom again."

"I have a key," Doug yelled from across the room.

110

Walking as casually as I could, I came up to Doug and put my hand out for the key. He grinned and gave it to me. I hurried over to the restroom, giving the door a couple of loud knocks, and finally used the key. I was shocked to find Howard on the toilet, pants up, head resting on his chest. If he was breathing, it was shallow.

My breathing stopped altogether as I reached for his wrist. It was cold and at first I didn't feel a pulse. Finally, I found a weak one. I backed out of the tiny room and tried to yell for help. My voice failed me. It had gone somewhere else, probably hiding in fear. I ran back to the main room.

"Call 911!" I screamed. "Howie's unconscious!"

Alicia backed two steps down, forgot the last step and landed on her rear. "Ouch! Don't worry!" she said, pulling her phone from her pocket while she sat on the floor.

Doug was quicker. He ran to the back room as he punched in the 911 operator. Alicia and I followed him. "Yeah, he's alive, but he's all beat up," he said. "No, I don't know what happened to him, but tell those guys to hurry." He stayed on the line, answering questions for several minutes.

Alicia lifted Howie's eyelids and felt his chest for a heartbeat. She rolled up his shirt sleeves and pant legs to see if he had needle marks or had been bitten by something. But the only visible signs of serious misconduct were the black eye and broken nose and those things had happened several hours ago since the blood was already dry and dark.

We heard sirens and hurried back to the main room.

One paramedic wearing a backpack looked around.

"Hi, my name's Josephine. Howard's back there," I pointed toward the kitchen. "He's in the bathroom," I said, as the young uniformed man took long strides while I ran beside him. Poor Howie hadn't moved. The paramedic did all the same things Alicia had done and more. Another medic arrived with a cart full of gear and a collapsible stretcher.

I backed away, not wanting to slow them down.

A few minutes later, Howie was rolled out of the building wearing tubes in his nose.

Alicia sighed as he rolled by.

I wondered who would do that to Howie, and why.

"Jo, give me Howie's card with Dolly's number on the back. I'll call her."

"Good idea," I said, and handed over the ranger's card.

That night I dreamt I was in a line-up at the police station. Alicia stood next to me and Howard and Dolly were further down the line. On my other side was the Roaring Camp Sheriff and a little lost boy dressed in rags.

I was shocked when the little boy was picked out of the line-up as the murderer. He foamed at the mouth and showed his large pointy teeth. That's when I realized he was a rabid dog. We all clung to each other in a circle while the dog snarled and kept us under his control.

Alicia led us in song, but I panicked because I couldn't remember the words to "God Bless America." Solow remembered the words and howled them at the little boy-dog until he melted into a puddle of rancid oil.

CHAPTER 11

Thursday morning, I was off to a rough start after nightmares and not much sleep. Still a bit groggy, I called Dolly. She answered after several rings. "Hello, Josephine…I'm rather busy at the moment, but I've already told Alicia everything. Goodbye, dear," she hung up.

Alicia must have called Dolly at the crack of dawn. I almost felt resentful—but not quite. Alicia was just concerned about Howard, like I was. A few minutes later, she called to tell me that Howie was recovering from the beating. The police were investigating and Dolly planned to take the day off to be with her son. Alicia said she'd drive herself to Felton because she wanted to shop after work.

I saw that as an opportunity to take Solow to work with me.

With my calls out of the way, I set about getting ready for work. After my shower and a hot cup of coffee, I slipped into my paint outfit for the day. While Solow and I ate breakfast together, I wondered how life would be when David and I were married. Would Solow still be important to me? Would I still love him? Would David still love his finicky feline?

Solow was unusually thirsty after I shared my omelet, fried potatoes and Portuguese sausage with him. He emptied his bowl of water. I refilled it.

I went to the bedroom to put on another layer of clothes since the Rec Center had no heat. Just in case, I gathered up a spare sweater, a pair of knitted leggings and a knitted cap for later if needed.

When I came back to the kitchen I found Solow in my chair with his front paws on the table. He'd eaten most of the dried apricots David had given me for Halloween. My fiancé had wanted to prove to me that there were plenty of sweet substitutes for candy. But I'd held firm in my claim that chocolates were health food.

When Solow finished lapping up his second round of water, we climbed into my little truck and cruised halfway through Aromas.

I heard something.

"Was that you?" I asked Solow, as he stared out the window.

I didn't expect an answer, of course, and I didn't expect him to heave his breakfast all over my passenger seat right there at the stop sign in front of the Aromas Grill. Quickly, I made a right turn and parked next door to the restaurant. I opened the passenger door and Solow leaped to the ground. I looked the other way as he cleaned out his belly in the flower bed bordering the outdoor patio where people usually ate when the sun was out. Fortunately it was early and no customers were eating outside at the time.

A man wearing reflective bomber sunglasses waved to me from the patio.

I looked up at the man thinking I knew him from somewhere.

"Josephine, it is I, Roger," he declared as he leaned against the wire fence and pulled his glasses off.

"Hi, Roger. I'm glad it's you. This is so embarrassing."

He looked at the open door on the truck. "That's quite a mess you have there. I will get some wet towels." He turned toward the entrance to the Grill.

"Roger, what are you doing?"

Over his shoulder, he said, "Do not worry, I work here."

A couple minutes later, he came back with several wet hand towels and a bottle of beer. "Do not worry; I left a few towels for the restaurant," he laughed, as he walked down the sidewalk straight to my truck. "Guess you will not be wearing these things," he said, holding up my knitted collection of extra clothing. "I will take them home and wash them."

"You're too sweet. Thank you, Roger. By the way, did I hear you say you're working here?"

"Yes, it is my first day. I set up the tables and chairs and umbrellas, then I scrape the grill clean and make the lemonade. I am doing physical labor here because I need to earn money and pay David back for all he has done for me. Eventually, I will rent a place of my own I suppose."

"I wouldn't be surprised if they make you head waiter within the week."

Roger smiled.

Solow sniffed the length of the garden, acting like his old self.

Roger scrubbed and cleaned the passenger seat and then the floor carpet. When everything was as clean as possible, under the circumstances, he opened the bottle of beer, took a swig and sprinkled the rest on the seat and floor.

"What...?" I gulped.

"Would you rather smell throw-up or beer?" he asked.

"I see what you mean. Thanks again, Roger,"

He spread a clean dry towel across the seat and helped Solow climb up onto it. At last we were on our way. Too bad it was too cold to put the windows down. I never did like the smell of beer.

After fifty-five minutes in light traffic, we rolled into Felton. I parked next to Alicia's Volvo SUV and helped Solow to the ground. It was a sunny day but lacked warmth. Looking to the far side of the parking lot, Howie's ranger truck looked sad and neglected. I wondered how the ranger was doing. But most of all, I wondered why someone would pummel a nice guy like Howie.

Solow led the way into the Rec building, inspecting everyone in it. When he came to Alicia, looking warm in her yellow jacket and dark green leg warmers, he'd found his heaven. She stopped mixing paint and gave him a good rubdown.

"I smell beer," she said.

"It's a long story."

"It's okay; I like the smell...just so he doesn't become an alcoholic," Alicia laughed, as she scratched Solow behind his ears.

We studied my sketches plus a few photos of the actual Roaring Camp town, and taped the photographs to the wall. We ignored ten feet of meadowland on the left side of the mural. Instead, we concentrated on how we'd finish up the landscape. Once the basic topography was established we'd create twenty feet of western style buildings.

"Jo, do you think Howie will go home from the hospital today?"

"I think so. There isn't much they can do for a broken nose and ribs."

"I think we should..."

"Visit him?" I said.

She nodded, and the painting moved forward even though poor Howie was on our minds. We did our job, carefully replicating the landscape. Once the hills and meadows were completed, I saw that we were at a perfect break time. We gathered our purses and walked to the front door with Solow leading the way.

Doug rolled his eyes, "Banker's hours?"

"We'll be back," I laughed. We left the building to Doug and two other carpenters. "Allie, did you talk to the two guys remodeling the kitchen about Howie's beating?"

"Actually, I did talk to the tall one. He said he had no idea someone was in the restroom. The workmen use the portable blue outhouse behind the building. He acted really shocked when I told him about Howie."

We climbed into our seats. Solow scooted under the dash, keeping Alicia's feet warm.

I fired up the engine. "What about the other guy, the one with the black whiskers sticking out his nose and ears?"

"Jo, look out!" Alicia said, watching Howie's truck, driven by an older man wearing a black baseball cap shoot across the parking lot from our right side.

I slammed my foot on the brake as the pickup passed in front of us and turned right onto Highway Nine. I had intended to turn left, but my unquenchable curiosity kicked in and I cranked the wheel to the right instead. We followed the green truck as it headed south on Highway Nine. Just half a block before the 'Deer Crossing' sign, the ranger truck turned right onto San Lorenzo Avenue.

"What are you doing?" Alicia growled as I cranked the wheel and turned up the narrow lane.

"I'm following Howie's truck, of course."

"Well, as snoops, I guess that's what we do," she admitted. Alicia calmed herself by looking out the window at a neighborhood scattered with homes at the end of long driveways half-hidden behind trees and natural foliage.

Howard's truck disappeared around a bend. I tried to catch up but it rounded another turn and disappeared completely.

"He's gone!" I hit the steering wheel with my palm.

"Go back and we'll take another look," Alicia said, leaning forward in her seat.

Intending to turn the truck around, I backed into someone's unpaved pot-holed driveway. In the course of pulling off that maneuver, I had to look in the rearview mirror. Just twenty yards behind us sat the green truck. Mr. Black Cap climbed out of the driver's seat, walked past an old rusty red compact car and marched up to a modest two-story country home built against a steep forested hillside. Like frontline soldiers, a battalion of odd-sized potted plants had been stationed across the width of the front porch.

I backed the truck up and tooted the horn.

The man turned around.

We waved at him out the windows.

Feeling the excitement, Solow howled.

Mr. Black Cap sauntered down the driveway and over to Alicia's window. "Ma'am, what can I do ya for?"

"We were following Howie's truck…" I explained.

"Oh, you gals know my son?" He grinned with delight as drops of chaw ran down his bristly chin.

"Does that mean that Dolly is your wife?" Alicia asked.

"Well, she acts like she's my wife," he laughed.

Alicia mustered a little chuckle, making him think he was on a roll.

"Yep, we got lucky and produced a fine boy. My name's Rory."

"Rory, we know that Howie's in the hospital. Can you tell us how he's doing," I said, as Solow pushed his way up to Alicia's window and poked his nose out.

"Nice dog ya got there."

"Thanks. We're worried about your son…"

"Oh yeah, that. I expect Howie'll be up and chasin' them nurses in a day or two," he said, as more brown juice ran into the patch of white and grey chin whiskers.

"Rory, do you know who beat him up?" I asked.

"Coulda been anybody. It's not easy bein' a forest ranger these days, what with murders and such goin' on."

"No idea?" Alicia said, as Solow finally was able to poke his whole head out the window.

"If you think of anything or hear about something, please give me a call," I said as I passed my business card to Alicia. She handed it to Rory.

He squinted his small grey eyes, holding my card at arm's length.

"There was a guy creepin' round our neighborhood last week," Rory said, looking up at the sky. "He was a stranger, taller than me, wearin' fine clothes and all, but not dressed for wet weather if ya know what I mean."

With trepidation, I remembered that my aunt and I had found Roger just a few blocks away from Dolly and Rory's home one week ago. Roger fit Rory's description. There might be a connection, but I couldn't imagine Roger creeping around anybody's neighborhood. I was still trying to sort it out when Alicia suggested we grab some lunch.

"The Taqueria here in town's great," Rory said.

We thanked him and I drove us directly to the Taqueria at the other end of town. Outside the restaurant Solow shared a sunny patio with half a dozen birds. He quickly vacuumed up all the spilled taco bits and pieces under the tables before the birds could get to them. After ordering inside, Alicia and I sat at a table in the sun and waited for our lunches to arrive. It was worth the wait.

"Jo, this burrito is divine."

"Can't be as good as my tostada," I said, using my napkin to wipe a splat of sour cream off my shirt. We were able to enjoy our lunches because Rory had set our minds at ease, mostly. Howie would recover. I didn't think about the Roger connection until much later when I was on the last mile of my journey home. Next to me, Solow flapped his paws as he dreamt, probably about a certain prissy white cat. My mind pondered the whole Howard situation. But pondering didn't help. Nothing made sense.

As I drove up my driveway and parked, a flood of warmth and love passed through me. Yellow light shone from every window and a thin curl of chimney smoke rose up into the starry sky.

David greeted us at the door. The moment was everything I imagined it would be.

"Josie, I thought I'd surprise you with a homemade dinner," he said, wearing his favorite BBQ apron Aunt Clara had given him for his birthday.

"Aren't you cold?" I laughed.

"Don't worry; we'll keep each other warm." His embrace proved the point. An hour later, we sat down to dinner, tired and hungry.

Solow had patiently waited for his dinner plus anything that might drop on the floor.

As David carved the roast chicken, he cleared his throat, "Roger had a breakthrough today."

"Really? That's wonderful."

"Well, it's a start. We were watching an old movie on TV about Evita Peron in Argentina. All of a sudden, he starts laughing. I asked what was so funny because I didn't see anything funny about the movie. He says it's funny because Peron is his family name."

"That is a breakthrough!" I was thrilled.

"When I left the house, Roger was on my computer looking up people with the last name of Peron. He's pretty excited. He called me about every five minutes while I was over here cooking, coming up with new internet searches. I hope he finds something."

"How does he like working at the Grill?" I asked.

"They already have him doing their books. There was an issue with a beer delivery. He glanced at the paperwork and told them the deal. Even I knew he was way too good to be pushing tables around and washing dishes. The man is comfortable on the computer and so far he remembers four languages—Spanish, English, French and German."

"I think we'll miss Roger once his memory comes back and he goes back to his old life," I said.

David nodded.

"How was work today?" he asked.

"We finished the background scenery and drew in the basic shapes of the buildings. After we 'paint the town' we'll paint the water tower and the steam engine. Did you know that Dixiana was the first steam engine Roaring Camp purchased? She's number one, but they have several other really old locomotives, too. It's kind of exciting when the whistle blows and steam shoots out all over the place.

CHAPTER 12

Kyle revved his Honda motorcycle one more time Friday morning as he pulled to a stop in front of the Felton Rec Center. I stopped in the doorway, turned around and watched Kyle dismount. He looked like a long-legged spider with a big yellow head. He yanked the helmet off and unsnapped his leather chaps. He wrapped his jacket around the pile of leather safety accessories and stowed it all on the shiny wood floor next to our painting equipment. He stood beside me, ready to paint.

Alicia was already in position to paint her section of wall.

"Like, how's the murder mystery going?" Kyle asked.

Before I could answer Kyle, Alicia said, "We're getting closer every day." She wasn't smiling and her tone was dead serious. For the first time I understood how close to her heart this whole fiasco was. It wasn't a game or a past time; it was family and it was serious.

We took our places in front of the wall. At the far left end, Alicia drew with chalk and then painted a quaint covered bridge built over a duck pond at the park entrance. Kyle stood facing the middle of the wall replicating Bret Harte Hall. I worked on a building to his right, Georgie's Cook House.

My section of the painting included train tracks disappearing into the lower forest. Later, I added tracks winding up Bear Mountain, always being consistent with my partners when it came to color and style. When painting buildings we used levels and rulers to draw straight lines and good perspective. We mixed our colors to match the barn-reds, mossy-greens and sunrise-yellows of the actual town.

Doug wasn't around and neither were his two sidekick carpenters. I wondered if Friday was a holiday.

Lunchtime finally arrived and the three of us decided to sit on our tarps and eat the lunches we'd packed.

"Where's your lunch, Kyle?" Alicia asked, knowing that he usually depended on handouts from us. As usual, he thankfully accepted the half sandwiches we gave him. When the three of us had devoured every last crumb, Alicia asked if I wanted to go look around Felton with her.

"Sure," I said, hearing something in her voice that indicated she had an ulterior motive. As per her instructions, I drove Alicia a few blocks to the other end of Felton. We passed by quaint storefronts offering things like ice cream, hardware, acupuncture and Chinese food. She pointed to a jewelry store she said she wanted to visit. I parked the truck and we found ourselves in a wee little shop smartly fitted with counters and cases of fine jewelry.

Alicia produced the lovely watch, bracelet and ring from her bulging pants pocket.

The woman behind the counter, wearing magnification head-gear, had saucer eyes as she held her jaw stiffly in place.

"Oh my God! These are copies. Right?" she swooned.

"That's what we're here to find out," Alicia said.

The woman ran her hand over the bracelet as if it were the soft belly of a little kitten. "Would you like to come back later?"

"No, we need to know right away," Alicia said, her voice intense.

The woman, looking as curious as we felt, grabbed her loupe and briefly examined the bracelet. A minute later, she dropped into the nearest chair, breathing hard, eyes blinking. She opened her mouth to speak, but only a squeak came out. She cleared her throat while Alicia and I held our breath.

"Ladies, we are looking at high-quality rubies, emeralds and sapphires." The bracelet shook in her unsteady hand. She looked at the stones again and shook her head. "It's unbelievable! And the setting is very old."

"Do you mean old like a hundred years?" Alicia asked.

The woman shook her head. "Older. I don't know exactly…" she sputtered. She handed the bracelet back to Alicia, turned and eyed the watch and ring lying on the counter. She hesitated, as if she didn't know which item to pick up first. Finally she chose the watch.

I listened to my heart beat and tried to remember to breathe.

Alicia seemed to be doing the same thing.

"This watch is not as old, but it has at least two carats worth of exquisite diamonds as you can see." She ran a finger around the dainty watch face and turned it over and read out loud the teeny-weeny words on the back, "Mi Amore," and the numbers, "2-10."

"I tried to read the back," Alicia said, "but it just looked like tiny dots. Thank you for reading it to me. It was my sister's watch and now I know there was romance in her life." Alicia brushed a tear from her cheek, took back the watch and handed the woman the last piece of jewelry.

Using the magnification she wore on her head, the jeweler leaned in to the ring for a close look. Suddenly she pulled back, both hands trembling.

"What's the matter?" Alicia asked.

"It's a perfect pink diamond," she stuttered. I've never seen one in person, only pictures. Without weighing it, I'd say it's around three carats."

"What does that mean in dollars?" I asked.

"At the very least, close to a million...could be a lot more depending on its history and other factors. That's for the pink diamond alone. The setting is worth quite a bit with those lovely little matching diamonds and the nineteenth century style gold filigree. I have to say, I've never seen such a lovely ring."

Alicia leaned against the counter looking like a raindrop could topple her over. She asked how much she owed for the evaluation.

"No charge. It has been the thrill of a lifetime seeing a large pink diamond. Would you mind if I took a picture of the ring? My boss will never believe it."

Alicia pulled up the sleeve of her yellow jacket, slipped the ring onto her ring finger and held her hand out.

The woman snapped a picture using her phone. "My husband will never believe this," she laughed.

I went from disbelief, to excited, to scared for Alicia. Was Maria murdered for her jewelry? Now that Alicia had the jewels, was she in danger? Driving the six blocks back to the Rec Center felt more like a hundred miles. Every car, every person along the way looked suspicious. Would the jeweler show the picture to her boss, her husband and other people? How could I keep my friend safe?

"Jo, you're so quiet. What's going on?" Alicia asked as we painted.

"I've been thinking about the jewels…"

"What jewels?" Kyle asked.

I looked around the room to see if anyone else was listening.

Doug had finally come to work after a dental appointment. I heard his skill saw grinding away on a shelf building project in the other room.

"It seems Alicia's rich," I whispered.

"Yeah," he looked at me, "I knew that. What's the big deal?"

"Kyle, there's a big difference between making a comfortable living and having a ton of extra money."

"Jo, it's not money; it's jewelry and I might just keep it," Alicia said, adding another shadow to her covered bridge. "It'd be like an insurance policy or an investment, always increasing in value. Besides, I don't think I could part with any of it."

"Where are they now?" I asked.

"Right here in my pocket."

"We need to do something clever to hide them."

"Hide them from whom?" she laughed.

"What if your sister was murdered for her jewelry?"

"Jo, I have everything—why didn't they take it from her?"

"Don't forget, it was dark and there were lots of people in the train cars. Even the murderer wouldn't know exactly where she landed." I glanced at Alicia and realized I'd said too much. In her fragile state of mind she wasn't ready to be reminded about the details.

At that point, we quietly concentrated on our painting. That was until Doug came into the room with a question.

"Anybody lose this hair thingy?" he asked, holding a hair clip out for us to see.

My heart skipped a beat, but poor Alicia looked like she might collapse. The clip looked old, gold and full of little diamonds. I knew that none of it was fake, but Doug didn't know that. He held the clip in his hand like it was his grandmother's bra. I was pretty sure he'd rather be holding a black widow spider.

Alicia's mouth opened but nothing came out.

I quickly composed myself, stepped away from the wall and said, "Thanks, Doug; it must have fallen out of my hair. Where'd you find it?"

"Behind the toilet."

I slipped the lovely Spanish-style, fan-shaped clip into my sweatshirt pocket.

Doug looked at me and cocked his head as if to say, "Yeah, it really goes with your painty t-shirt, scruffy old Levis and that worn out sweatshirt you're wearing." But he didn't say it out loud. He just turned and walked back to his project mumbling to himself.

Kyle kept painting, oblivious to the emotional state of his female partners.

"Allie, I have something in the truck I want to show you," I said.

She put her paint brush in water and followed me outside where I handed over the clip.

"Where should I put it?" she asked, still looking stunned even though she'd only glanced at the clip once.

"How about in your glove compartment? After all, you keep your car locked."

Alicia considered my advice and pushed the clip into her pants pocket. She marched back into the building and pulled her car key out of her purse.

I painted while she stepped outside again.

A minute later she was back.

"Everything okay?" I asked.

Alicia nodded and turned her back to me.

"The clip looks great in your hair, but…"

"Don't worry, Jo, I'll lock it up when I'm ready. I'm feeling my sister's love right now." Her eyes were red-rimmed and moist. She played at painting but didn't accomplish very much. I didn't say anything because I knew she was struggling to hold herself together.

Kyle, on the other hand, accomplished a great deal. When he'd finished painting his second building, he asked if he could leave a little early. His girlfriend was making dinner for him and he needed to go home to shower and shave off a week's worth of fuzzy red beard.

Smiling to myself, I wished him well and sent him on his way.

It was late afternoon. Solow finally woke up from his nap and I knew he was in need of a walk. I hooked his leash to his collar and off we went, leaving Alicia to hold down the fort. We walked a couple blocks north. Solow peed on a tuft of grass growing through a crack in the sidewalk and then artfully watered two tires on a parked Subaru.

As we passed an ice cream shop window, someone inside caught my attention. I recognized the jeweler. She was talking to a spiky-haired man with broad shoulders, wearing a black jacket. I couldn't see his features because he sat with his back to the window. His precision haircut seemed out of place in the casual country town of Felton. I hoped he was her boss but doubted it.

Walking felt good so I decided to go two more blocks and turn around at the jeweler's shop. The shop was closed. A note on the door read, "Be right back."

As we turned around to go back to the Rec Center, the jeweler came hustling up the sidewalk and gave us a cheery greeting. She admired Solow and chit chatted like we were lifelong friends. A gust of cold wind hit the back of my neck. I told her we had to get back to the Rec Center right away, but breaking away from her one-sided conversation wasn't easy.

"I hope you'll drop in at the shop again sometime," she said, whipping out a business card for me. She said her name was Olga Fenway. Just then a stiff breeze blew her half-black, half-grey hair into a frizzy bush. She smoothed it down and then told me all about her hairdresser's unlucky marriage and divorce.

"Thanks, Olga, we really have to go. We'll probably drop in again sometime." I didn't mention the clip, feeling like her loose lips wouldn't be helpful. They might even be dangerous. How many people had she told already? But there was always the off-chance she was a real professional and hadn't told anyone about the jewels.

As we approached the Rec Center, Solow put his nose to the ground and howled.

"What was that for?" I said.

There were two more howls as we walked past Alicia's car and my truck.

Doug's truck and Kyle's motorcycle were long gone.

Solow and I entered the immense, noiseless space newly configured for indoor basketball. Every footfall echoed. I didn't see Alicia and figured she was probably having a smoke in the bathroom to calm her nerves. I painted highlights on the train station and added grassy patches along the tracks.

Ten minutes later, I checked my watch. I figured Alicia must be on her second cigarette but that was a ridiculous thought since she could barely stand a few puffs of tobacco smoke. It was four-thirty, with another cold winter night fast approaching. The best thing for Alicia would be for her to go home and relax. I marched over to the far end of the backroom where the only operational restroom was located, and noticed the door was ajar.

"Allie?"

I peeked in. Empty. I headed back to the mural.

Thinking Alicia might have stepped outside for some air, I began cleaning brushes and stowing paint equipment against the wall. When that was done, Solow lumbered over to the door as he usually did when he knew it was time to go home.

But Alicia still wasn't around.

There was only one thing left to do, call Alicia's cell phone.

She didn't answer her phone.

I waited five minutes and tried again. No answer.

Suddenly I felt like I couldn't breathe. My heart pounded frantically.

Solow and I circled the building and found nothing. Unless Solow's enthusiastic sniffing of the far end of the parking lot meant something.

CHAPTER 13

Friday night lasted for an eternity. My first call had been to 911. The sheriff was prompt and enthusiastic. She followed Solow around the grounds, shining her flashlight into every dark corner while I tagged along making two more phone calls.

My second call, Ernie, was extremely painful for both of us. He said he'd be in Felton as soon as possible. My third call went to David. I tried to be stoic but began sobbing as soon as I heard his gentle voice.

"Ma'am, excuse me." Ms. Sheriff stood beside me.

"Goodbye, David. I have to go."

"The only thing I can see is that your dog continues to sniff the ground over there at the far end of the lot. I've already called in for more help, so take it easy and take a few breaths. We'll get to the bottom of this. Is there anything unusual or suspicious you'd like to report?"

"Actually, there is something," I sniffed, "Alicia's sister, Maria, was murdered Halloween night at Roaring Camp."

An eyebrow went up as she pulled out a note pad and wrote a couple quick lines. "Anything else?"

Should I say anything? I asked myself. Finally, I decided I should tell the officer about the jewelry. "Alicia had her sister's jewelry in her pocket..."

The officer's attention switched to an incoming vehicle.

A siren went silent. Two male officers climbed out of the official sheriff's SUV. A German Shepard sat at attention in the back of the vehicle.

The woman officer told me to put my dog in my truck.

While I hiked Solow into the passenger seat, the three officers went into a huddle to see what the next play would be.

Forty minutes later, Ernie arrived in his Toyota sedan with Trigger sitting wide-eyed in the back seat. I hugged Trigger and told him the officers were there to make sure his mother was located as quickly as possible.

"That's my mom's car," Trigger pointed to the Volvo. "How do you know she's missing?"

I leaned down, hugged him again and said, "We don't know if she's missing. We don't know anything yet. But I know we'll find her. Why don't you sit with Solow in my truck for a while?"

"Sure, unless you want me to help," Trigger offered.

"The officers will take care of that," I said, walking him over to the truck.

Ernie had been invited into the police huddle. He brought with him one of Alicia's scarves for the dogs to smell. My heart went out to him as he answered their questions.

I stood near my truck in case Trigger had a meltdown.

David's little Miata roared into the parking lot. He slid it into a space between Ernie's car and my truck, climbed out and held me for a moment while his eyes searched the area. His caress caused me to suddenly let go of all the tears I'd been holding back. When they finally stopped, I shivered. He wrapped me in his jacket.

"Josie, do you mind if I go offer my help?"

"Of course not," I said, minding a great deal where my own comfort was concerned. But volunteering was absolutely the right thing to do—anything to get Alicia back! I wanted to help with the search, but I knew that Alicia would want me to be with Trigger.

Another siren cut through the cold dark night, and went silent. Two deputy sheriffs climbed out of their squad car and joined the huddle. Time seemed to stretch into eternity. Finally, the meeting broke up. I watched five officers and two volunteers follow one German shepherd heading west along Highway Nine.

I climbed into the driver's seat of my truck, turned on the engine and cranked up the heater. Trigger wore a jacket, but looked like he was cold.

Solow was asleep on the floor under the dash, but Trigger was wide awake and full of questions I was unable to answer. He mentioned he hadn't had dinner yet, so I turned off the engine, left Solow in the cab and we walked two blocks into town to the Chinese restaurant. I planned to order several entrees in case Ernie, Alicia and David came back starving. Surely they'd find Alicia soon. I tried to remember what she was wearing besides her usual paint clothes. Her yellow jacket wasn't in the building so I figured she must be wearing it. That would mean that she meant to go outside for some reason. Had she been looking for me? I shouldn't have left her alone.

Our waiter spoke perfect English as he greeted us and reported the soup of the day. I asked if there was MSG in any of the food. Suddenly he had an accent and a hearing problem. We were hungry so I ordered mountains of food for myself and my ten-year-old companion plus several take home dishes.

The waiter-owner hustled back to the kitchen.

"Auntie Jo, are you worried?"

"A little bit," I admitted, trying to be honest, but not wanting to worry Trigger. One of the greatest things about Alicia was her son, the son I never had. I had no children from my long ago marriage and it was obviously too late to have them with David. All I could do was enjoy Trigger.

We sat side-by-side facing two large windows, watching Felton transform itself from a bustling mountain town into a sleepy after dark little berg with just enough street lights to serve all four blocks of town. Commuters were still passing through the main intersection on their way north to Ben Lomond and Boulder Creek, both towns serving as bedroom communities for Silicon Valley.

Eventually, Trigger fell asleep in his chair. I left him alone as long as I could, but the waiter kept looking at us. He'd stripped the table down to just one plastic bag containing four little white boxes of food and my receipt.

Staring across the street, a group of people caught my eye. I leaned forward, straining to see who was in the parade following a big black German shepherd. Five flashlights were aimed at every dark corner, alley and parked vehicle. I watched as they crossed the main intersection and headed down to my window.

"Hey, sweetie, wake up. Let's go see your dad."

Trigger took a deep breath. "My dad...where?"

"Let's go outside and catch up to him."

Our waiter looked relieved as we filed out of the restaurant onto the side walk. He quickly flipped the *open* sign to *closed*.

David, Ernie, and the deputies, led by a German Shepherd, marched down the sidewalk ahead of us.

Trigger ran yelling, "Daddy, Daddy!"

Ernie stopped and turned around just in time to haul Trigger up into his arms briefly.

Carrying a bag of food had slowed me down but I finally caught up to Ernie. His sad eyes told me everything. They hadn't found anything to go on. We stood shivering in the Rec parking lot, listening to one officer telling us they'd keep in touch with us and that an all-points bulletin had been sent out. They suggested we put up posters with Alicia's picture.

"What about a daylight search party?" I asked, wiping tears away.

"It's already being organized for tomorrow," the woman officer said.

I busied myself at the center, shutting off lights and locking doors.

As the official vehicles drove away, my heart shattered. How could the world go on without my friend? How could I comfort Ernie and Trigger when I couldn't open my mouth without choking on my sobs?

David was sensitive to my unhinged condition and told me he'd drive me home and back to Felton the next day to pick up my truck. I wasn't sure I'd be ready to drive, but I set that worry aside. Sitting next to David in the warm cozy Miata finally took the kink out of my neck and stopped the flow of tears from sore eyes.

Sleep was the only relief from conscious worry. Even my dreams tormented me. Just when a speeding locomotive was inches from running over me, I woke up in a sweat. I looked out the passenger window at winking stars above dark neighborhoods. My fuzzy brain tried to step away from the scary dreams, but I couldn't shake the feeling of fear. As the miles slipped by, I was thankful to have David at the helm and Solow at my feet.

As the Miata roared up Otis, I asked David to take me to his house instead of mine. He didn't say a word, just parked in front of his ranch-style home and helped me out of the car. It was ten-thirty and icy cold. We hustled up to the fully lit front porch with the new motion sensor light Roger had recently installed.

Solow took care of business and climbed the three wooden stairs to the front door. Ms. Fluffy must have jumped out of bed on the wrong side (her usual), hissed and swatted Solow on his nose as he entered the house.

I headed straight for the couch, pulled a lap blanket over myself, clothes and all and fell asleep—but not before I felt a gentle kiss on my cheek.

My first sensory awareness the next morning was the smell of coffee and the sound of bacon frying. An unidentified feeling of sadness filled my being and sucked my energy. Red-eyed and pale, I visited the bathroom mirror. Yikes! I splashed my face with cold water, squeezed toothpaste on one finger and rubbed it across my teeth. I ran fingers through my tangled hair and finally ventured out to the kitchen where Roger made waffles and David made the Mimosas.

"Good morning, beautiful," David said.

"Good morning…I guess," my voice went down to a whisper as scenes from the night before flashed before my eyes, like Alicia telling

138

me the jewelry was in her pocket and would be fine. It wasn't fine, she wasn't fine—nothing was fine.

"What do you take on your waffles?" Roger asked me.

"I don't care, whatever's around."

"Josie likes whipped cream and berries," David said to Roger. "I'll start the scrambled eggs."

Usually I loved the sight of men wearing big aprons while cooking good food, but that morning I just wanted to be left alone. Even the smell of bacon couldn't make me happy or keep me there. Like a Zombie, I walked out into the chill morning air and headed home for a hot shower.

Solow stayed with David. I didn't even care. One more male not to worry about.

Beyond miserable, I flopped down on my couch and fell asleep. The dreams were less weird and more clear than usual. The one I remembered best was the one with Roger leading a pack of search dogs. I watched him as he looked up and saw Alicia swinging from tree to tree. Her face changed slightly and became Maria's face. Roger and David argued whether it was one sister or the other.

The doorbell rang.

Experiencing a knee-jerk reaction to the door bell, I rolled off the couch and stood up. Blinking and rubbing my eyes, I looked around the room trying to shake feelings of gloom from the last dream.

The doorbell rang again.

I opened the door.

"Roger? What are you doing here?"

"David thought maybe you didn't want to see him," he said, in his enchanting accent. He handed me one perfect red rose obviously picked from David's rose garden.

"Good grief, I'm acting like an idiot. Sorry, Roger, I'm just so concerned and upset."

"I know you are, and I'm sure David knows that." He started to leave, then turned around. "Did David tell you I've remembered a few more things?"

"No...that's wonderful!"

"Yesterday I was standing in David's apricot orchard when suddenly I remembered picking oranges as a young boy. Someone had given me permission to pick from their tree. I took the oranges home to my family...many little children. I remember that day because I had to walk to the far side of the city where I'd never been before and climb the orange tree. It made me feel older and very important. I can still see my mother's smile when I gave her the oranges."

"What was the name of the town?"

Roger thought for a moment. "It was...it was..."

"Don't worry, you'll remember everything," I said, as a couple of ideas popped into my head. Considering Roger's accent, his home town was either in Mexico or some other Spanish-speaking country. If we could only find Alicia, she might be able to help Roger remember where he was from. But how to find Alicia? I'd gone over that problem a hundred times in my head already.

As soon as Roger left, I dragged my lethargic body into the shower. Once I was clean, I paid special attention to my hair and makeup. I took the rose with me from room to room, a reminder that I should try to be a nicer person around the man I loved. Even as I thought about my beloved, the phone rang.

"Josie, I just heard from Ernie. He wanted to know if we could stay with Trigger while he goes up to Felton."

"David, I have a better plan; ask Roger to watch Trigger while you and I go to Felton."

"But…"

"David, you know I have to be there. She's my dearest friend."

"I knew you'd insist," he said, sounding defeated. "I'll ask Roger and see if that works for him. Might be fun for Trigger to practice his Spanish with Roger and keep his mind off his mother."

David called later to say that we'd be dropping Roger off at the Quintana home. Trigger's grandmother would also be there, convalescing.

Once Roger was dropped off at the lake house, David's old four passenger Jeep rumbled and bumped its way north on Highway One to Felton. Solow slept on the back seat while weekend traffic moved sluggishly along. It was less troublesome than the regular commuter traffic but probably seemed slower because of my impatience.

David parked the Jeep in the Rec Center parking lot several yards away from three canine units. Solow ignored the units and anointed Doug's truck tire. He joined us as we stepped into the building.

Doug walked up to us. "Hey, Josephine, too bad about your friend."

"Do you know where the search party's gone?" I asked.

Looking like he just fell out of bed, Doug tugged on his chin for an answer. "I don't know where they're going. I watched them leave the parking lot heading west on Highway Nine a couple hours ago."

"Thanks, Doug."

I was out the door on his last words.

David caught up to me. "Josie, you know there isn't much we can do."

"I don't know any such thing. I have to try to find Alicia," I said as I fast-walked west along Highway Nine with Solow leading the way.

One miserable mantra ran through my head, "If I had only stayed with Alicia, nothing would have happened to her."

CHAPTER 14

Rustic little Felton boasted modern concrete sidewalks lining its main street as far west as the Rec Center, where concrete turned into a dirt path alongside Highway Nine. Solow and I hurried down the path, our eyes smarting as bright mid-morning sunlight blinked through holes in the forest's green canopy. Dodging the occasional downed limb, rivulets of rain water and uneven ground kept us engaged. David must have lost concentration for a moment when he tripped on a couple of small branches taken down by the recent winter storm. He leaped over the first one but didn't see the second. Or maybe it was a pinecone he rolled his foot on.

"Josie!" he yelped.

I stopped walking, turned around and looked back ten yards.

"What happened?" I asked, as I hurried to where he sat on the ground holding his bad ankle.

"Can you help me up?"

"I'll try," I said, pulling on his arm.

"Just bend over; I'll put my arm over your back and then you straighten up." That sounded easy. But it wasn't.

"I think I better go back and get my truck," I said, wondering what else I could do.

"No, bring the Jeep," David said, handing me the keys and warning me about second gear, the one that didn't connect easily. We were less than a half mile from the Rec Center, but way too far for a twisted ankle to go. I handed Solow's leash to David so he wouldn't be alone while I jogged up the highway to get the Jeep.

The Rec building was as deserted as the parking lot, except for Doug. I approached him, told him what had happened to David and asked if he'd help load David into the Jeep. Doug put down his power screwdriver and followed me outside. I climbed into the driver's seat and stared at the dash. It was uncomplicated but unfamiliar at the same time. Worse than that, my experiences with shifting had been limited.

Doug sat next to me studying the interior of David's old, but nicely kept Jeep. I'm sure it was a "man thing," to lust over a mechanical item like that. He cranked his head around and asked me what that big black thing in the back seat was.

I turned and looked. "Oh my gosh! It's David's boot from the last time he twisted his ankle. That's why he asked for the Jeep." Suddenly I was so happy I almost cried. All I wanted to do was drive quickly over to David but first gear wasn't easy and second gear was impossible.

Doug looked at me like he wanted to take the wheel or at least plug his ears but that wouldn't be a manly thing to do. In my experience, guys are supposed to like ugly, grinding noises.

"Now that it's in second gear, I'll just keep it there," I said, "it's not far."

Doug said something under his breath and I was glad I didn't hear it.

We hugged the edge of the road and let the light traffic pass us. With David finally in sight, I pulled the Jeep to a stop at the side of the road, moving forward as close to him as I could. I helped David strap on the boot and Doug managed to get him upright and into the passenger seat. Doug and Solow settled into the back seats.

"I'm sorry, Josie; I know how much you wanted to join the search."

"Don't worry, David; let's get you somewhere comfortable."

Doug leaned forward, "There's a chaise lounge in the kitchen. Seems like it's always in my way. I could set it up for you."

"Thanks, buddy; that sounds good," David said, his voice sounding a bit hesitant to me.

"And I have a tube of arnica gel in my purse from the last time you wrenched your ankle," I said. Minutes later, David sat in the chaise lounge under a basketball hoop. I gently rolled his sock down and slathered arnica on his ankle. I let the cool gel soak into his skin for a few seconds, pulled up the sock and reinstalled the boot. I adjusted the chaise lounge so that David could stretch out but was not completely flat.

"Take it easy, old man," Doug quipped. He handed me the keys to the building saying he'd be back Monday. I dropped them into my pants pocket.

"Thanks, Doug, for the help," David said.

Dabbling at the mural, I watched David out of the corner of my eye. Sure enough, he finally relaxed. His eyes closed and his head lolled to one side. I quickly washed my brush and shrugged on my beige down jacket with rusty brown faux fur around the hood.

I hooked Solow to his leash and we left the building. Trotting along the side of the highway heading west, we had to stop to let horses go by at the corner of San Lorenzo Avenue. I noticed the familiar "Deer Crossing" sign a few yards past the street sign.

"Hi, Solow!" Grace shouted from her saddle.

Solow howled.

"Hi, girls. Have you seen a forty-year-old woman with black hair wearing a yellow jacket?"

Grace leaned toward me, "We haven't seen anyone on foot."

"Thanks; enjoy your ride."

The girls trotted across the highway where they entered Cowell State Park.

"Should we stay on Highway Nine or turn up San Lorenzo?" I asked Solow, who was still watching the girls on horseback as they disappeared into dark woodsy shadows. He began pulling on the leash in the direction of the highway. Since he was my very qualified sniffer dog, I let him lead me as far as the deer sign where he began plowing through old wet leaves with his nose. Solow suddenly stopped and looked up at me. Something in the leaves sparkled. I bent down and retrieved a gold cufflink featuring a solitaire diamond.

Shivering in the shade, I realized I was standing on the exact spot where I'd found Roger. I knew he wore expensive clothes, but diamond cufflinks? Did anyone still wear cufflinks? Solow and I spent another ten minutes shuffling through the mulchy leaves looking for anything shiny.

When I was one hundred percent sure there was nothing else to find,, I tugged on Solow's leash, encouraging him up San Lorenzo Avenue. After a few turns in the road we came to Dolly, Rory and Howie's house. I noticed that the ranger truck was sidled up to a retaining wall at the edge of a grove of redwoods and laurel, about twenty feet from the house—not where Rory had parked it two days ago. The other two cars were missing.

I decided to go see if our friend Howie was home from the hospital and if he was, I'd ask him if he had any information that would help us locate Alicia. Solow pranced up the driveway to the hillside home where all but two rooms were located on the top floor. We climbed a dozen or more wooden steps to the long front porch.

A squirrel chattered as he ran along the railing.

Solow pretended not to see him.

Above us, threatening clouds moved into what had been blue sky just minutes before.

I knocked on the front door a couple times and peeked in the big front window. There was no sign anyone was home so we turned to go down the stairs. On the way, my foot knocked over a potted succulent, one of a couple of dozen plants all facing west. With my hands, I scooped up as much dirt off the deck as I could and put it back into the righted pot. My eyes stung as I thought of Alicia who never accidentally knocked things over.

A jay squawked, another answered and a gust of wind rustled dead leaves across the driveway. I heard a branch snap somewhere in the forest. Suddenly, I felt like calling to Alicia, but on second thought that sounded silly.

Solow and I plunked down the steep stairs. At the bottom, he pulled on his leash with force. I followed the pull as far as Howie's truck where Solow sniffed the passenger door like it was a New York steak.

"So, what about the truck?" I said to Solow.

He lifted his leg and gave it a squirt.

"Didn't your mother teach you not to piddle on ranger trucks?"

I pulled him away and we marched to the end of the driveway.

"Right or left?"

Solow turned around and pulled in the direction of Howie's house. Finally, I gave in, deciding to let my sniffer dog take us wherever he wanted. Back at the green pickup, Solow thoroughly smelled the front and back bumpers, fenders and tires.

The squirrel chatted us up from a branch overhead.

Solow pulled in the direction of the squirrel.

"Wait, Solow, where do you think you're going?" I yelled, as my semi-athletic dog hopped a row of rocks lining the driveway, yanked the line out of my hand and disappeared into the dense forest. I rushed after him, staying as close as I could while encountering all the low-hanging branches that he didn't have to dodge. Miscalculating the height of one branch ended with my hair in its clutches. I worked hard at untangling myself, scoring hand and facial scratches as I worked. Even as I broke away, several twigs stayed nestled in my hair.

Solow howled once, twice, three times.

A jolt of emotional electricity coursed through my body. Was he on Alicia's trail? I knew the general direction the howl came from. There were many little pathways and none of them were easy walking-crawling. Solow's intermittent howls kept me focused in his direction. All I had to do was crawl on my hands and knees through the underbrush, imagining spiders and ticks falling into my hair. The path finally opened, letting me walk upright for a few yards and then it was back into a tunnel of foliage.

"Solow, where are you? We need to go back...David will be worried."

That message bounced off Solow's pointy head with zero results. My dog wasn't about to turn around. He knew his duty and he was doing it, howling every minute or so. I admired his endurance but swore I'd put him to bed without supper if he didn't stop and let me rest. Finally, he did stop. Still crawling on my hands and knees, I came face-to-face, rather face to doggie rump, with Solow panting at the edge of a clearing.

I stood up and looked up.

A giant spreading oak held its mighty branches up to the darkening sky.

A few drops of rain plunked down on my face.

As I studied the tree's magnificence, I noticed a well-built child's tree house nestled into the heart of it. The small house was made out of wood painted dark green, making it barely visible from the ground.

As I stood staring at the little treehouse, I thought I heard something metal clink against something metal.

Solow sniffed around the tree, ending on the far side where a rope ladder hung. He howled mournfully, the howl he uses when he's found something.

I ran to his side and looked up the ladder to a small door.

Rain splattered my face.

I decided to climb the ladder since I'd spent a good part of my life climbing ladders, but this one gave me a fight. It twisted and turned until I got the hang of it. By that time I was at the top rung, stretching one leg onto a mini porch with no rails. As I pulled my other leg up, I stared at a padlocked door in front of me. Naturally, I planned to retreat. I had one leg in the air searching for the rope ladder when I heard the metal-on-metal noise again, but louder.

Deciding I was hearing things, I put my foot in the rung.

"Clink."

I pulled my leg back up onto the porch. "Hello?"

"Clink."

"Who's in there?" I shouted.

"Clink, clink, clink."

That wasn't much of an answer, but it was enough to keep me interested. I crawled around the narrow three-sided porch looking for a way in. On the North wall I found a small window and peeked inside.

Raindrops multiplied into a downpour. Even with my hood pulled up, I was being drenched. On the ground below, my poor Solow had no cover as he sat quietly on wet leaves.

I looked through the window a second time. The boxy little room was flooded with dim light playing off cobwebs and thick dust. It all shouted, "Nothing to see here."

Trying to keep from slipping off the narrow, 'slick-as-snot porch,' I bumped my head on something that clinked. I crouched down closer to the floorboards, cranked my head around and looked up at a silver wind chime featuring six little metal raccoons. They moved side to side gently in the wind. Just as I decided to climb down from my perch, I saw two raccoons clink each other. Maybe it was a wind chime 'high five.'

Feeling foolish and defeated, I hooked one foot and then the other onto the ladder rungs. A few steps down, I hit the ground like a wet sponge. All that, and still no sign of Alicia.

Solow stood up and howled for me to follow him.

"How can I believe you?" I said to the wind.

Solow howled again, long and hard, so I followed him. Forward couldn't possibly be as bad as going back through low tunnels of sticky bushes. I figured we were headed north again judging by the fluorescent green moss growing on the backside of the tree trunks.

The forest quickly gave up to open rocky land, a couple houses in the distance and a well-worn path. Solow veered left onto a wide horse trail, or so it seemed from the piles of manure. Nose to the ground, he sniffed his way over to San Lorenzo Avenue where we made another left. I followed the leader as he trotted on bouncy legs all the way down to Highway Nine. My trotting energy was long gone, but the gentle slope kept me going as I managed to keep Solow in sight.

Before we turned left onto the highway, I looked to my right at the "Deer Crossing" sign. Suddenly, I had a convergence of consciousness. It occurred to me that I was searching for three things—my best friend, her brother and Roger's identity. There was the coincidence of Roger being found near the deer sign on Highway Nine and Solow leading me into a nearby neighborhood in our search for Alicia. I didn't believe in coincidences and suspected that Roger, Alicia and her brother Del were all connected somehow.

Still walking along the edge of the highway, I tried to remember Alicia's brief description of her brother. And then it hit me. I remembered seeing Roger's shoes after David had cleaned the mud off of them. They were huaraches! The same type of shoe that Alicia mentioned her brother had worn. That was it! Roger no doubt was actually Del! I couldn't wait to get home and tell him who he was— or who I thought he was.

I burst into the Rec Center dripping wet, but exhilarated.

David looked up from his chair, "Can you help me to the restroom?", he said flatly.

I quickly peeled off my jacket and walked him up and over to the restroom at the back of the building. On the way back, I explained all that had happened on our search, ending with my epiphany.

David sat on the edge of the chaise lounge and smiled. "That makes sense. Roger will be very happy to finally know who he is."

"Yeah," I said, "now if only I could find Alicia and tell her."

CHAPTER 15

Sweet and sour emotions, prophetic and puzzling thoughts ran through my head Sunday morning as I re-capped Saturday night from my warm bed. David and I had finished each other's sentences at Saturday's supper in his dining room. Del, better known as Roger, ate his rib steak with tears in his eyes as David told him about his sisters. The poor man chewed the same bite slowly for a very long time. He finally swallowed and wiped away tears with his napkin.

"This does not come as a complete surprise." Del said.

"What do you mean by that?" David asked.

"Remember when you picked me up at Alicia's house?"

David and I both nodded.

"Trigger had been showing me a big family picture album. You and David always called his mother Allie. When I saw pictures of her, much younger of course, I thought of Alicia. I asked Trigger to describe his mother's car. His description matched the green Volvo I remembered seeing when I met with her at the cafe. So many things were popping into my head."

"That's wonderful, Roger, I mean Del. Can you remember who was chasing you and why?" I asked. "I think Allie might be involved with the same thug."

"I will tell you if I am able to think of it," Del said, rubbing his brow.

I spent half the evening talking to Del about Alicia, hoping something would jog his memory. He did remember having diamond cufflinks and he remembered having an apple pastry with his tea at the cafe. Maybe everything else was too awful to remember.

Our plan for Sunday was to drive to Felton and join the search party at 10:00 a.m. in front of the Rec Center. I offered to drive since David's ankle was still hurting. In the end, he declined to go, saying his ankle needed more rest. I knew it was killing him not to go. He was as anxious to find Alicia as I was. The new plan was for Ernie and Trigger to meet up with Del and me in Felton. Trigger would be another set of eyes and ears.

I'd just finished eating breakfast when Del arrived at my house. Dressed in our warmest jackets, we quickly piled into my truck. Solow crawled under the dash for his first nap of the day. Because it was Sunday with clear weather and light traffic, we arrived in Felton early. I parked my truck several yards away from two Sheriff's SUV's, each with a dog in the back.

Del, Solow and I walked up to a cluster of sheriffs and volunteer citizens bent over a folding table studying maps. When the lady sheriff looked at us, I introduced Del as Alicia's brother. That got their interest since yesterday I'd told her there were no siblings to help search.

"This is good," the female sheriff said to Del, "sometimes family members can be a big help."

"I will try very hard to find her," he said.

She turned her flushed face back to the maps, obviously dazzled by his good looks.

I gave the sheriff the key to the Rec Center and we helped move the table inside just in time to avoid a light sprinkle blowing in from the north.

Del and I inched closer to the table as volunteers crowded around. The sheriff must have felt our breath on the back of her neck. She turned around and invited us to study the maps and handed each of us a red plastic bag.

Four just-arrived volunteers pushed in behind us trying to see the maps.

The deputy sheriff cleared her throat, "Don't forget to take pictures as you go. If you find an item that you think might possibly pertain to the hostage or the perp, put that item in your red bag. We'll analyze the contents later."

The word "hostage" shot painfully through my heart. Reality was a bear.

Three more volunteers arrived and half a dozen after that. We were pretty evenly split with thirteen males and eleven females, until Ernie and Trigger walked in. Ernie was all about business. He couldn't look at me without his eyes brimming with tears and it was the same for me. Just when I thought I didn't have any tears left, my eyes sprung another leak. It was the hug from Ernie that did it.

Ernie and Del went outside to talk.

Minutes later, Ernie walked in with his arm over Del's shoulder. If only Alicia could have seen them as brothers-in-law.

Trigger spent his time teaching Solow new tricks like *stay* and *howl* on command.

Representatives from the local TV station, KPUT, arrived in a van outfitted with an assortment of antennas and dishes. A surfer dude cameraman and a young woman learning how to be a newscaster took pictures, interviewed several volunteers and summed up the sad situation for the viewers. That was the last we saw of them.

Half an hour had passed since we'd arrived in Felton. Finally we were shown the areas to be searched on a new set of maps. Search areas were ringed in red ink. We were encouraged to form groups of three or four. Naturally Ernie, Trigger, Del and I stuck together. One deputy checked us out and thought it would be a good idea to have Solow go along. As if I'd leave him behind. Obviously he was our biggest asset.

We were assigned the day use area at Henry Cowell State Park. It seemed like a good place to look since the park's picnic area was just a mile from the Rec Center (as the crow flies) and shared a boundary with Roaring Camp. We were instructed to search the extensive day use picnic area and meet back at the Rec Center in three hours.

Our party piled into Ernie's little Corolla. He drove Henry Cowell's flat windy two-lane road deep into the park and then turned right onto a narrow road leading into the day use picnic area. We passed by a couple of parking lots but Ernie chose to park his car in the last lot, closer to the river. The picnic areas were scattered along both sides of the road. A lot of territory to cover.

Climbing out of Ernie's car, I stepped onto mushy wet leaves covering the earth. Bay tree aroma filled the air as shy squirrels and birds scattered, leaving us to our work. Ernie, and Trigger looked glum but ready to search. Like spokes on a wheel, we spread out in four directions. Solow stood for a time trying to decide who to follow. He finally chose Trigger, as any sensitive comfort dog would.

It would be three more months before Feltoners and tourists could expect to enjoy their sunny picnics again. In the meantime, the place was chilly and dead quiet, but at least the rain clouds had vanished and the wimpy November sun shone as best it could.

After carefully sizing up three picnic clearings, each one with its basic barbecue, cold water faucet, trash can and picnic table with built-in benches, I finally found a little something. It was only a crumpled tissue, but Alicia always kept one in her jacket pocket. I put it in my red bag.

Tromping over uneven ground to another picnic sight with the same basic accommodations, I discovered fresh tire tracks. Someone had obviously passed up the parking lot and parked their vehicle a few feet from one of the picnic tables. An empty Cheetos bag had fallen short of the large metal trash can. I stuffed the bag into my red bag, not really sure why. I pulled out my cell phone and took several pictures of the tire tracks.

Trigger and Solow caught up to me.

"Find anything, Trigger?"

"Not really, just this…" He handed me a white lunch bag with orange taco grease and salsa smudges on it. A stash of used wadded up napkins had been stuffed inside the bag. "It was the only thing in the trash can," he said, as he ran off to be with Solow.

Expecting the bag to smell bad, I held it under my nose with two pinched fingers. Surprisingly, it just smelled like chicken tacos. "Kinda heavy for just napkins," I mumbled, reaching my hand into the bag while Trigger threw a stick to Solow.

"Oh my God! She was here!" I choked, staring at a bracelet, a ring and a watch. If I turn this stuff in to the sheriff, how do we know that Alicia will get them back? I thought about it for one second and quickly dropped the handful of jewelry into my pants pocket while the boys ran in circles around a giant big leaf maple.

Del walked up behind me.

I twirled around, red-faced with guilt.

"What's the matter, Josephina?"

"Nothing." I straightened my jacket. "Solow and Trigger found this bag. I smelled it and it doesn't stink. I think someone was here recently."

Del put the bag up to his perfectly arched nose and sniffed. "This is a worthy find," he said, almost smiling. "At the edge of the clearing I saw footprints. Would you like to take a picture?"

My heart did a double thump. "Of course." I followed Del a few yards over to the foot prints. Parts of Saturday had been wet and stormy. It looked like at least two people had walked across Saturday's mud, leaving a couple large shoe prints and a few smaller ones. As I snapped pictures, I tried to remember the shoes Alicia wore the last time I saw her. The only thing that came to mind was the cold, cavernous Rec room where I'd left her.

In the distance a train whistle blew.

Solow howled.

I checked my watch. It was almost twelve-thirty, almost time for the Roaring Camp train to leave the station. I silently wished there had never been a train circling Bear Mountain. That was where the bad luck had started, but where would it end? I thought of the victims—Maria, Del, Howard and Alicia.

"Del, later today we should check on Howard. He's the ranger who went aboard the train that you were on."

Del tilted his head slightly, his eyes looking off to the right at nothing.

"I have a fuzzy memory of a man wearing a green ranger uniform talking to Maria. Another man pushed the ranger and told him to leave the lady alone."

"What did the other man look like?" I asked.

"It was getting dark…he wore a dark coat…and he looked angry. I think I knew him. Yes. Now I remember! He worked for Maria's husband, Enrique!" Del rubbed his forehead, trying to bring up more memories. The full impact of Maria's death seemed to hit him for the first time. His dark eyes went darker as he clamped his mouth into a hard line.

I had so many more questions for Del. But before I had time to ask, Ernie joined us with news that he'd just checked out the restrooms across the road. In the lady's room he found the word, "help" scratched on a metal door and fresh footprints in the mud outside. I wondered if Alicia had walked in mud on purpose, hoping to leave prints for someone to find.

We searchers converged, shared what we'd seen and decided we had plenty to tell the sheriff and the sooner the better. When we got back to the Rec Center, only one sheriff and her volunteer husband had stayed at the command post. They were discussing the mural when we walked in with our findings. Once we had their attention, we shared what we found, including a picture Ernie took of the bathroom door.

"Anyone could have scratched that on the door," Ms. Sheriff said.

"What about these fresh tire tracks and the footprints?" I asked, as I showed the pictures on my phone and then presented her with the white lunch bag.

"From the Taqueria," she said. "Lots of people eat there."

It was all I could do to keep from rolling my eyes.

"I need to have the pictures from your phone," the sheriff said, scooping up the white bag and the red bag for further study.

"Sure, just tell me how to send them to you."

"I'll take care of it," she said. "Hand me your phone."

I handed over my phone. Should I give her the jewelry? I tossed the idea around as I watched the sheriff approach a young couple coming in the door, each carrying a red bag stuffed to the brim. Like mine, their phones were temporarily confiscated for their pictures.

My insides shouted, "I know it was Alicia because I found her jewelry."

After mulling over the problem, I finally sidled up to the sheriff.

She finished transferring the pictures and turned her head, "Yes?"

"I, ah, forgot to show you this," I said, pulling Maria's watch out of my pocket. "It was in the Taqueria bag."

"Do you know who it belongs to?"

"It belongs to Alicia. It used to belong to her sister, Maria, who was killed two weeks ago."

"Thank you. I'll tag it. Here's your phone."

"It's worth a few thousand...I know Alicia wants it back."

"Don't worry; we keep good records," the sheriff said, as she dropped the watch into a Manila envelope and labeled it with a Sharpie. At least the precious watch wasn't dumped into a red bag full of rotting garbage.

Ernie and Del volunteered for the next search which was scheduled for three o'clock. The men thought Trigger and I should go home and rest—that whole, "women and children thing." Ugh! But I wished them luck anyway.

Trigger, Solow and I climbed into my truck and headed into Howard's neighborhood. There was something about San Lorenzo Avenue that tormented me. In my head I planned to drive past Howard's place and check out the other end of the road. But, being a rather flexible person and female, I changed my mind.

I parked my truck beside Howie's ranger truck and behind an older little reddish car plastered with faded bumper stickers, including one from Roaring Camp. Solow opened one eye but Trigger kept his shut. They were exhausted. I climbed out of my seat, closed the door quietly and strolled over to the staircase.

"Hey, Josephine, whatcha doin?" Howard said.

I turned my head and saw Howard standing behind a half-open window on the first floor.

"Howard, I need to talk to you."

"Go that way and I'll let you in," he said, pointing to the corner of the house. I rounded the corner just as Howard opened the side door. He escorted me down a short hallway to his bedroom and pulled out a wooden stool from his very retro desk for me to sit on.

"Thanks, Howie." I sat down. "Did you know that Alicia is missing?"

He instantly paled. "That's awful. What happened?"

"I wish I knew. Friday she was alone at the Rec Center and when I came back, she was gone. Have you seen her in the last twenty-four hours?"

"Gosh, no…where could she be?" He scratched his head as his freckled brow scrunched in the middle. "I was kinda under the weather myself."

"Yeah, what happened to you? Who left you in the restroom?"

Howard's cell phone rang. He looked at it lying on his desk but left it alone. Next to the phone was Maria's face on the front page of the *Sentinel*.

"I recognized this big guy creepin' around the back of the center," Howard said, "so I started to follow him to see what he was up to. He entered the building through the back door. I opened the door to go in, but he was waiting for me…with his fists. He flipped me in the air. He just kept pounding me. I didn't have time to defend myself; in fact, I was barely able to get to the bathroom and lock the door. The next thing I know, I'm getting a ride in an ambulance. I still have a concussion and my ribs are killing me."

"Do you know this guy?" I asked.

"Not really, but I did see him on the train Halloween night and I picked him out of a lineup for the cops."

"What does he look like?"

"Big thick guy, but a little bit shorter than me…with black spiky hair and a scar on his cheek."

"What does he drive?"

"I don't know for sure, but there was a white van with Oregon plates parked in the lot." Howard looked at the floor.

"You have my card, Howie. Call me if you remember anything else."

"Sure, no problem."

"That's a nice treehouse you have."

"You saw my treehouse?" He looked surprised.

"Actually, I was looking for Alicia when Solow took off into the woods."

"Yeah, that could happen…" he mumbled. "What are you going to do next?"

"I don't know. I just have to keep looking for Alicia." Dang, the tears stung my eyes again. I noticed Howard's bloody tee shirt at the top of a pile of dirty clothes, and looked away.

CHAPTER 16

Leaving San Lorenzo Avenue Sunday afternoon, I turned right onto Highway Nine and made a left one block later. The entrance to Cowell State Park was beautiful and frightening to me. How could terrible things happen in such a lovely setting?

I parked my truck in the upper parking lot.

Trigger woke up and looked around.

"Wow, are we going on the train?" he asked.

"Sorry, the train already made its run for the day. But I thought we could look around."

"Great! Come on, Solow; it'll be fun!" Trigger said, as he clambered out of his seat holding Solow's leash. Suddenly, he stopped, his face fell and tears streamed down his cheeks. I put my arm around his quivering shoulders and waited for the sadness to be released.

"I miss my Mommy..." he stammered.

We held onto each other, hearts breaking, until the tears finally stopped.

Solow was up for whatever Trigger wanted to do. He pulled on his leash. They ran ahead, leaving me to lock the truck. I hurried across the lot and fast-walked up the path, trying to catch up to the boys. Up ahead, I saw Trigger talking to a park ranger. When I finally caught up, Trigger introduced Ranger Clancy to me.

"Wonderful dog ya got there," the ranger smiled.

"Thanks. Have you seen a forty-year-old woman with shoulder length black hair in a pageboy cut? She's about this tall?" I put my hand up to my own five-foot-six height. "She was wearing a yellow jacket."

"I'm sorry, ma'am; I just got here, but I'll keep an eye open."

I handed him one of my business cards.

He shook hands with Trigger, tipped his hat to me and walked away.

"Let's go to the General Store, please, please..." Trigger begged.

We stepped over the railroad tracks, crossed the wide dusty street and entered the old fashioned store.

Dolly looked up from her knitting. "Well, what do you know, it's Solow and Joan..."

"Josephine, and this is Trigger."

Trigger smiled politely and headed for the displays of train books at the back of the store.

"Handsome little devil," Dolly commented.

"His mother's missing," I said, trying to sound normal.

"I heard about that. She's your friend?"

I nodded, "Alicia."

"Alicia's a very nice lady," she said. "I heard they're sending out search parties today."

"Yes, they are."

"What can I do to help you, dear?" Dolly said as she put down her knitting needles.

"I have some posters," I choked.

"Don't worry, I'll put them up around town," she promised.

Handing her half a dozen posters, I asked Dolly if she'd seen anything suspicious.

"No, I'm afraid not. It's been very quiet for a Sunday."

"I'll try to enlist Howard's help when he's feeling better," I said.

"Are you meaning he'd do that in an official capacity?" Dolly squinted her eyes.

"Being a ranger, I figure he can…"

"Not really, my dear, you see my son only acts like he's a ranger."

"I don't understand," I stuttered.

Dolly took a deep breath. "He graduated from college and took the ranger training but the state never hired him. There are so many qualified people wanting to be rangers that not everyone gets hired. It's been six years."

"How is it that he wears the uniform and drives a ranger truck?" I asked.

"The good folks running Cowell Park and Roaring Camp don't mind having his help. He wears a green shirt and pants but it's not the official uniform. The badge comes from here," she pointed to a shallow little box full of shiny silver badges. "His friend, Clancy, lets him borrow the truck." Dolly shrugged, "My son's happy, but I do wish they'd pay him."

"How does Rory feel about that?"

"His stepfather doesn't understand, but then, they've never been close," Dolly said, with glassy eyes. "Rory grinds his teeth every night in his sleep over the fact that his stepson works for free."

"I kinda see his point," I said, imagining the man asleep with tobacco juice staining his pillow.

Dolly smiled, "But Howie enjoys certain perks like riding the train and free admission to the park and twenty percent off the price of anything in this store. He loves Roaring Camp. He does a lot of hiking, you know." A couple of dimples drilled into her pudgy cheeks.

"Is Howie still suffering from the loss of his wife and baby?"

Dolly's dimples disappeared as her cheeks went red. She stared at the counter top. "He tells people that story because he thinks he should be married by now." She reached down and stroked Solow's velvety ears.

Dolly had shocked me with her words. What a sad story!

Trigger sidled up to me, holding a book about trains.

"You're going to read that whole book?" I asked, knowing that he was a very capable reader for ten, when he felt like reading.

"I'll read it, Auntie Jo. Mom would want me to."

I paid for the book and we left the dimly lit, all wood store quickly. My eyes stung all over again as late afternoon sunlight shot into my corneas. Everything was blurry, even the blocky guy with spiky black hair holding a newspaper in front of his face. He followed us about thirty yards down the street and positioned himself behind a family standing directly behind us, as we watched the horseshoe demonstration.

A mustached smithy dressed in 1880's garb pounded iron while I covertly glanced at the crowd behind us. It was an interesting demonstration, even though I'd seen it before, but my mind was fixed on the blocky guy behind us. For the moment, my concern for our safety had been placated by the fact that we stood with a large group of people.

Trigger had seen enough and wanted to go next door to the museum.

I stalled, not wishing to leave the crowd.

Solow pulled on his leash. I finally gave in and we walked a few yards over to the museum. Unfortunately, it was closed. A yellowed note on the door read, "Happy Halloween."

"Halloween was a long time ago," Trigger grumped.

I agreed and turned to go, but a blockish man stood in my way.

My blood froze. Was I a coward or just overly imaginative? I decided to confront the man. "Are you following us?" I finally blurted out. "Where is Alicia?"

"No habla Ingles," he muttered, as he turned and walked away.

We walked quickly in the other direction, heading for the parking lot. The sun had just dropped behind the western mountains and instantly the air went from cool to cold. I shivered and pulled my jacket tighter at the collar.

Trigger ran circles around me, followed by Solow. They innocently gamboled their way across the parking lot, as I watched "Mr. Block" out of the corner of my eye. I herded the boys into the cab of my truck, leaped into the driver's seat and quickly locked the doors.

Off to my left, I noticed Mr. Block getting into a white van with Oregon plates. Imagining Alicia tied up in the back, I let him drive away first. I followed at a modest distance. My next thought was, what can I do if I catch up to him? I have a dog with me and that's good, but I also have a young boy to look after.

Mr. Block turned right onto Highway Nine and one block later he turned left onto San Lorenzo Avenue.

Even though my heart pumped double time, I resisted turning up that familiar road. I'd save it for another day. Poor Ernie would be home soon and wondering what had happened to Trigger. The man had enough to worry about with Alicia missing.

Trigger and Solow quickly fell asleep giving me much too much quiet time to think. For the hundredth time I prayed Alicia was alive and well. My thoughts bounced from Alicia to Del to Ernie to Trigger. Did they blame me for leaving Alicia alone at the Rec Center? I blamed me and it hurt.

It was dark when I we left the highway and drove through Watsonville. The driver of a chopped Honda revved his motor in the lane beside me. When the light turned green, he flew over the crosswalk while I slowly cruised through town and into the Lake District. In the dark I saw lights reflected on the pond surrounding the Quintana's house. I parked across the street. Failing to wake Trigger, Solow and I climbed out of the truck and came back with Ernie. He scooped Trigger up in his arms and carried him into the house.

Tired and hungry, I wanted desperately to be home but decided I needed to talk to Ernie first. Trigger woke up hungry and half an hour later we were all eating cheese quesadillas, including Solow, and drinking cinnamon flavored hot chocolate. Ernie's cooking skills were much appreciated by me. But I'd never seen him so quiet.

Trigger's head bobbed in the direction of his plate. It looked to me like he might face plant straight into the remains of his quesadilla. Ernie saw it too and walked Trigger up to his bedroom. When he came back, I told him about the white paper bag Trigger had found with a watch in it.

"Why do you think the watch belonged to Alicia?" Ernie asked. "She doesn't wear a watch—she has her phone."

"It was Maria's watch and it was in Alicia's pocket along with these," I said, pulling the bracelet and ring out of my pocket.

Ernie's eyes blinked. "That stuff isn't real...can't be."

"We took them to a jeweler and they're very real. They're not only real, they're flawless."

His jaw dropped. "You found those in a garbage can?"

"It's just lucky Trigger found the bag. I gave the watch to the detective, but not these," I said, handing over the jewels. "Mind you, they're worth ocean-front property, and that's why I didn't feel comfortable handing everything over to the authorities."

"I guess you did the right thing, Josephine. The watch is enough to show that she was in the picnic area. Maybe the detectives can take it from there."

"I hope so," I said, with more gusto than I felt.

"Trigger must have had a good time today," Ernie said, "he's exhausted."

"He's not the only one," I said. "Did you find anything significant at the park today?"

"Not really," Ernie said, "just tire tracks that could belong to anyone, and a blue scarf that I don't think is hers. She's not crazy about blue and I don't remember seeing it before."

"You're right; it doesn't sound like something she would wear."

"Del found a pile of beer cans," Ernie said, "probably from some under-aged yahoos."

"Have you checked your messages, Ernie?"

"Yes, I have. No ransom requests," he muttered.

"Ernie, you're not going to believe what Dolly told me today. I can hardly believe it myself. Her son Howard, the ranger, is not a real park ranger. His badge comes from the General Store and a ranger friend loans him the truck."

"You're kidding!" Ernie gulped.

"It's weird. Dolly says that the owners of the park are fine with Howard helping out here and there, but they never pay him. His stepdad isn't very happy about that."

"How does he live?"

"Pajama Boy lives in the folks' basement." I yawned, "It's only nine o'clock, but I'm beat. Time to go home, Solow." The dog didn't miss a snore. I leaned down and lifted one ear, "Let's go for a ride."

Solow perked up, stood up and howled.

"Quiet old boy; you want to wake up Trigger?"

I thanked Ernie for dinner and promised him we'd keep searching till Alicia was found. My words sounded hollow. Action was all that counted.

The light in Ernie's dark brown eyes had gone out. His whole posture spoke of a worst case scenario.

"Wow, Trigger sure can snore," I commented.

"That's not Trigger; it's Del. He crashed in the guest room as soon as we got home."

"How do you guys get along?" I asked.

"We get along like long lost brothers. He's my brother-in-law, and I'm glad he wants to live with us until he gets his new life together." Ernie opened the front door for me.

"Looks like your lake water is going down," I said, trying to leave on a positive note.

Clangor chugged away under a streetlight, belching fumes as it sent lake water two blocks over to the Pajaro River.

"Yes, it's gone down a couple inches," Ernie said, without enthusiasm.

"I hope you can help Del to remember what happened Halloween night," I said, over my shoulder as Solow and I walked out the front door and down the ramp.

"I'll work on it. Good night, Josephine," he said and closed the door.

Thankfully, Ernie had installed a shorter wider plank for people like me who might trip and topple into two feet of smelly lake water.

Already a thin line of scum ringed the exterior stucco walls, proof of where the water had recently been.

Once I was driving, a long train of thought kicked in. The thought-train reminded me that it was a good thing that Del was staying in Watsonville since he and Ernie were both hurting. They had known each other for two days but under extremely stressful circumstances. I figured Ernie would probably help Del to remember his past and Del would help Ernie find Alicia using recall information about Halloween night. I was dying to pump Del for everything he could remember, but it would have to wait.

Home had never looked so good. My sleepy dog lumbered into the house. David had a cozy fire going, while he dozed in front of the TV. Rather than wake him, I quietly fed Solow and checked my messages.

Clara had called. I played the message twice. She said she'd meet me at the Rec Center, tomorrow morning. I hadn't spoken to her in a while and wondered how much she knew about Alicia's disappearance.

I left Clara a message since she'd already gone to bed. Once that was done, I curled up on the couch next to David and fell asleep against his shoulder. I dreamt that Howard's family was having a picnic in the woods. Doug, Del, Alicia, Trigger, Ernie and David came to the picnic dressed as forest animals. Off to one side of the clearing was a large cage with bars. Behind the bars stood a blockish hairy animal with black spiky hair. The animal grinned when he saw me.

CHAPTER 17

In the wee hours of Monday morning I sent an email to the committee in charge of construction at the Felton Rec Center advising them that one of my employees, also my best friend, was a missing person and possibly being held hostage. Therefore, I was in no condition to paint. I added the fact that my other employee was already enlisted in the search party. I was sure they knew the whole story, living in the little Felton community, and I didn't care how they felt about it. I didn't care if the whole building fell into a sinkhole. I just didn't care about anything.

It was unusual for me to wake up early in the morning, let alone get out of bed before seven. By five o'clock I'd already showered, dressed, fed Solow and tossed a load of dirty clothes into the washing machine. I paced the floor and chewed my nails down to nubs. I packed a lunch big enough for a dozen lumber jacks and filled my biggest thermos with hot coffee.

When seven o'clock finally rolled around, I hoisted Solow into the truck and headed for Felton. I wore paint clothes under my warmest jacket in case we found Alicia and I suddenly felt like painting again. It was a long-shot since I had no clear-cut clues to follow, just a few hunches.

Upon arriving at the Rec Center, the first person I saw was Kyle shedding his helmet and chaps. We walked up to each other. Suddenly we had no words. We both loved and respected Alicia and that was communicated through two sets of glistening green eyes.

Looking around, I wasn't surprised to see Ernie, Del and Trigger hanging out at the far end of the Rec Center parking lot listening to a couple of deputies. Kyle and I joined the group of eight volunteers. Someone mentioned that more people were scheduled to arrive for the afternoon search party.

I raised my hand.

"Yes, ma'am?" the female officer said.

"If we're covering the San Lorenzo Avenue area..."

"It's been searched," she said, and continued pointing out circled areas on the map.

"Actually, Alicia could be anywhere by now," I mumbled, and regretted saying it when I realized Ernie was standing close behind me.

People were grouped according to transportation. Ernie and Trigger would go in the Toyota and Del and I would go in my truck. A young couple decked out in matching slug-yellow stretch pants and hooded jackets was all set to ride their bikes to the closest neighborhood.

Del and I walked toward the truck. "Oh my gosh, there's my Aunt Clara and Ben!" I waved to them in their white F150 pickup as it pulled up to the sidewalk a few yards away. Ben helped Clara down from her seat and we all came together on the walkway.

I introduced Del as Alicia's brother.

"Good to see you Roger, I mean Del," Aunt Clara said.

"Are there any new developments?" Ben asked.

"Nothing so far," I said. "Just go over to the deputies and they'll tell you what to do." I pointed to the table set up on the blacktop several yards away. "We'll see you here around noon." We hugged, and went our separate ways.

Del helped Solow back into my truck. We headed to our designated search area with high hopes and two red bags. Our assignment was to search the last mile of Toll House Gulch Road which turned out to be a beautiful but long mountain drive up a steep, narrow road with amazing views at times.

We decided to go to the end of the road and work our way back along our assigned mile. Nearing the top of the mountain, I saw a pull-over spot just before the road narrowed into a dead end driveway. I parked the truck. As soon as we clambered out of our seats, Del held one of Alicia's shoes under Solow's nose for a moment. Solow instantly had her scent and led the way. Del and I leaned into the wind as we trudged up a steep unpaved driveway. Even Solow slowed his pace.

Reaching the domed top of the mountain, we saw that several acres had been stripped of all trees. A small house centered in the middle of the bald spot sat bravely facing elements such as winter wind and summer sun. It reminded me of a wart on a bald head.

Del peeked in windows while I knocked on the weathered front door. A wild gust of wind tried to blow me off my feet and rattled my courage. No one answered the door. I circled the house with Solow and tried the back door where the wind wasn't as bad. Taking into account the fact that there was obviously no garage or vehicle around, I was ready to leave.

Del met up with us at the back of the house next to a six-foot high woodpile. A few feet from the pile was a stump with an ax stuck in the top.

"This would be a perfect place to hide," I said. "It's like another world up here, with endless redwood forest in every direction. But I think we're wasting our time."

Del agreed with me.

We'd just started walking downhill toward my truck when a black Camaro roared past us and parked near the front of the house.

We turned on a dime and headed back to the wart.

Ranger Clancy climbed out of his muscle car and greeted us with a wave and a smile.

"Hey, Clancy, this is Del and I think you know Solow."

"Nice to meet you, Del," Clancy said, as they shook hands. "And there's that great dog."

"That is a very beautiful car you have," Del replied.

"Thanks, buddy," the ranger laughed. "What are you guys doing way up here? This is for nature freaks like me."

"I'm in favor of nature," Del said, "but we're here on a very serious matter."

"Don't tell me you're looking for the missing woman." Clancy's smile quickly disappeared.

"Yes, we are, Clancy," I said. "and, coincidentally, Howie was beaten up the day before Alicia disappeared. I think it all ties in with Maria's murder."

Clancy lifted his ranger cap and scratched his head of receding blond hair. "You told me about the lady who's missing, but I didn't know Howie got pegged. Is he okay?"

"He has a concussion, broken nose and ribs but otherwise he's okay, according to his stepfather," I said. "I saw him, and he's doing fairly well."

"I'll give him a call," Clancy said. He wished us luck and turned toward his house.

With so much more territory to cover, we left without further ado. Once we were seated in my truck, I looked at the gas gauge and decided it was a pit stop we had to have.

Del began talking as we rolled down the mountain into Felton.

"Josephine, I must tell you that after seeing this lonely place on top of a mountain, it reminds me of my home."

"That's wonderful, Del. Do you remember where your home is?"

"I can picture it in my mind," he said thoughtfully. "There's water all around it. I can't quite name it, but it will come to me."

"Sounds like it's an island," I said as we pulled into a gas station.

"Yes, yes it is an island…very empty of trees with buildings in the middle." He almost smiled and then slipped back to his heartbroken demeanor. "I remember there was a time when my sister and I were happy to live there. Maria's husband Enrique was a gentleman, businessman and owner of the compound. Maria was treated very well until three years ago when Enrique brought a younger woman to the island." Del stared at Solow lying on top of his feet. "You see, Enrique wanted children and Maria couldn't…"

"Hang onto that thought," I said, as I climbed out of my seat, swiped my credit card and let my truck suckle up some gasoline. Climbing back into the driver's seat, I asked Del to continue.

"There's not much more to say, just that Enrique became a cruel and disloyal husband. Maria tried to leave the island but he had eyes and ears everywhere. A man who promised to help her was never seen again."

"That's awful! Was Enrique mean to you?"

"Not really; I pretended I didn't know what was happening. He depended on me because I took care of all his bookwork, finances, everything."

A horn tooted behind us.

"How did you and Maria escape?"

"Because of the work I did, I knew many vendors and visitors to the island. One woman, whom I liked very much and she liked me, arranged for us to leave on her boat which would be heading to California. We docked in San Diego and quickly arranged passage to Portland, Oregon, on a private yacht owned by well-to-do friends of ours."

"Why Portland?" The car behind us revved its motor. "Okay already!" I said to the rearview mirror and proceeded to park my truck at the curb.

"We had another contact there," Del continued, "and thought going to Oregon would throw Enrique's people off our trail."

"So you rented a van and drove down to Santa Cruz County to find your other sister, Alicia, right?" I pulled my truck into traffic.

"That is right," he said, "but soon we discovered someone was following us electronically. I had not realized that Maria still had her phone in her purse. After our meeting with Alicia, we left the phone in a trash can and drove into the Santa Cruz Mountains to hide."

"Why did you take a train ride Halloween night?" I asked, parking at the Rec Center and switching off the ignition.

"We did not even know it was The Day Of The Dead. We were being chased by someone in a black car so I drove into the park where there were many people. We saw official California State symbols on green trucks and thought we would find policemen there."

"So you got on the train hoping to get away from whomever was chasing you?"

Del stared straight ahead, unblinking. "After parking the van, my recollection is not very good." His chin dropped, eyes watering. "But I remember going into a store to buy a warm jacket for Maria."

The sky sneezed—a stiff wind shook the truck and seconds later a billion fine little droplets covered the windshield.

"Here we go again," I muttered.

"Better than having less than one inch of rain a year," Del said, as we darted across the lot and filed into the Rec building.

"It was a desert island?"

"Yes, you could say it was a desert island, but not every year was dry. Sometimes we were in the path of tropical storms. We could not depend on our reservoir for water. Some years we had to distill sea water into drinking water," Del said, as we walked inside and over to the map table. He handed over our red bags containing next to nothing.

Ms. Sheriff looked at the bags. "Not much luck?"

"No, I'm afraid not," I said. "We didn't have time to cover the whole area. It's pretty wild territory up there."

"Yes, I can see that it is. This afternoon we're putting you and your friends back on Toll House Gulch Road. There are parts not yet searched. Divide it up between yourselves," she said, and turned to the couple wearing yellow cycling gear.

"You look tired, Del," I said, as we headed for the front door with our new red bags.

"I am okay," he said, "I will do anything to find my sister. Look, Ernie and Trigger have arrived."

"Ben and Clara are here too," I pointed.

They burst through the door soaking wet. Trigger shook his head like a dog after its bath. Water went everywhere. The Rec floor was already slick from dripping wet people coming and going.

The canary yellow couple pulled up their hoods, rounded our little group and took off on their bikes. Wondering why they'd joined the search in such miserable weather, I watched them turn west onto Highway Nine. We followed them in our rain-proof vehicles until we came to the familiar Toll House Gulch Road. Ernie drove to his assigned section of street and Ben drove farther up the road to his.

Sitting in my parked truck at the entrance to Toll House Gulch Road, Del and I ate the sandwiches I'd packed. He left half of his corned beef sandwich saying he'd eat it later. I figured he was just too worried and sad to eat very much.

I climbed out of the truck, put up my hood and popped my umbrella open. Del put the hood of his borrowed jacket up over his head. Solow jumped down to the street where we carefully placed our feet between little rivers of rushing water, until it didn't matter anymore. No matter how hard we tried to stay dry, less than an hour later we were soaked and chilled to the bone. We persevered and searched our assigned six blocks with Solow leading the way. My knuckles were sore from knocking on doors. Every time a door opened, Del pulled a picture of Alicia out of his jacket and held it for the people to see. We searched their faces for clues. We searched their whole neighborhood for clues, but our little red bags came up empty.

Periodically, we sat in the truck with the heater on. Del didn't look good. His eyes were red and his face was pasty white. I finally decided Del needed to rest. We piled back into the truck just as Ernie drove past us heading to town. Trigger had gone into the search with enthusiasm but I learned later that he hadn't lasted very long. Damp, dark forests can be depressing.

I parked the truck at the Rec Center where a deputy came up to my window and asked for our red bags. I handed over the bags. Unfortunately we had nothing of consequence to tell him. We watched Ernie as he handed over his red bags and quickly drove away. He was emotionally unable to look our way.

By the time Del and I reached the Quintana house, Del was shivering uncontrollably. I perspired heavily, as the heater blew hot air into the cab.

Solow had slept peacefully until we arrived in Watsonville and it was time for Del to leave us. He climbed up into the passenger seat and watched me shout hot tea and hot bath instructions to Del as he walked toward the plank. He turned, waved and stepped onto the plank. His body leaned precariously this way and that but he finally made it to the front door.

Ernie opened the door and helped his brother-in-law inside.

All the way to the grocery store, I asked myself where Alicia was, always making sure I pictured her in my mind alive and well. Seeing the misery stamped on my face, Robert walked the aisles with me pointing out specials, telling jokes and trying to cheer me up.

"Josephine, after the search, where does your mind take you?" he asked, as he straightened a row of pickle jars.

"It keeps taking me to San Lorenzo Avenue."

"Why?"

"Because we found Alicia's brother near there and Howie lives on that street."

"Would you mind if I joined the search tomorrow?" Robert asked.

"That would be wonderful...but what about work?"

"I have sick days coming and I never get sick," he smiled.

I thought about Del and predicted he wouldn't be well enough to be in a search party any time soon. Suddenly I was overcome with gratitude, grabbed Robert and planted a motherly kiss on his smooth freckled cheek.

"I see we have good customer relations," the store manager said, as she passed by us on her way to the backroom.

Robert's face went even redder.

"Thanks for volunteering. See you at the Rec Center in Felton at eight," I said, as I hurried away with my cart half full.

As soon as I got home I unloaded the grocery bags and called Ernie. He told me Del was running a temperature and had gone straight to bed. Ernie wanted to know if we could team up on the next day's search. He planned to leave Trigger home with his grandmother and Del. I told him we'd be a threesome because of Robert.

With all that settled, I finally realized it was past dinner time. I had no appetite. Instead of cooking I called David and poured out my fears. Would we ever see Alicia again and so on until he cut me off.

"Josie, I know you're hurting. We all are. I'm going to go with you tomorrow and we're going to find Alicia."

"But what about your sprained ankle?"

"It's better...don't worry, I'll wear the boot." David's voice cracked. "I'll see you in the morning."

We hung up, as tears streamed down my cheeks. Everyone knows that the chances of finding a missing person lessen as time moves on. I heard it in David's voice.

My house was too quiet. I needed a distraction so I walked over to the TV for comfort.

Suddenly the kitchen phone rang, jarring me out of my dark thoughts.

"Hello, Auntie..." I said.

"Oh, my dear, you sound so sad. I called to cheer you up."

"I'm okay."

"Sure you are. Actually I have news that might help your mood," she chirped.

"Okay, I'm listening," but I was still hurting from my self-induced bad attitude.

"Well, after the second search, Ben and I checked in at the Rec Center and I watched a woman dressed in yellow bicycle gear hand over her red bag plus a piece of jewelry. Said she found it lying beside the road."

"What road, Auntie?"

"I believe she said it was San Lorenzo Avenue."

"And what did the jewelry look like?" I held my breath.

"I saw it in her hand. It looked like a beautiful little golden fan with sparkly diamonds all over it."

"Oh, Aunt Clara, Alicia was wearing that hair clip when she disappeared!"

"Oh my, this is good!" she said. "We'll scour that road tomorrow. Goodnight, my dear," she said, and hung up.

"Hang on, Allie, we're coming!" I said to the wall.

I drank a glass of milk and fell asleep on the couch with the taste of hope on my tongue.

CHAPTER 18

Monday night dreams melded into Tuesday morning nightmares. I dreamt that Alicia or Maria—I couldn't tell which—was trapped inside a little birdhouse that caught on fire. I wanted to stamp out the blaze, but I was afraid I'd crush my friend. Finally I knew it was Alicia when she began singing. She had a mic that sent her voice out to the world. The fire department heard her and rushed to the scene. When they arrived, the fire had already gone out, so they turned their hoses on me.

Slowly, I opened my eyes. Solow's wet tongue slid across my cheek again.

"Do you need to go out?" I asked.

He stared at me lying on the couch under a knitted afghan. Purposefully, he turned his head and looked at the front door. It was a hint I couldn't ignore even though it was still dark outside. Once Solow was out the door, I settled onto the couch cushions and pulled up the afghan for another half hour of sleep. But before I had time to fall asleep, Solow barked to come in.

It was still dark when I decided to get up and get ready for another day of searching for Alicia. When David, Solow and I arrived at the Rec Center, it looked like the whole town had turned out armed with umbrellas and flashlights. Fortunately, we didn't need umbrellas or flashlights as the sun came out giving me hope that something good would happen.

Spotting our little group of searchers standing at the far end of the parking lot near the highway, I kept going and finally found a parking space two blocks down the street. We walked briskly over to the little circle, David taking long clunky strides in his black boot as Solow bounced along.

Clara and I hugged. She quietly reminded me of the hair clip she'd seen the day before.

A deputy approached our group and showed us two circled areas on a map of Felton. Ernie thanked the officer and promised we'd search those areas. When the deputy left, I asked Ernie how Del was doing. He said Del was resting.

Clara and I looked at each other. "Ben, dear, do you mind if I team up with Josephine?" He smiled and rolled his eyes, acting like we girls would probably get into trouble but gave his blessing anyway.

"Oh, look," I said, pointing across the lot at two girls on horseback, one studying a map. "I'm glad to see teenagers getting involved. And look over there, it's Robert. He said he'd be here." I waved for him to join us.

"We'll take Robert and Solow with us," Clara announced.

"Wait a minute; my truck only seats two."

"No problem, Josephine," Robert said, "my car seats four."

Ernie, David and Ben teamed up and climbed into Ben's pickup. David scooted into the back seat, turned sideways and stretched his legs across the seat. We watched as Ben's truck led a whole parade of vehicles leaving the parking lot. Cars from a fast food parking lot across the street joined the exodus.

My team, led by Robert, marched up the street to the Taqueria parking lot.

"My what a spiffy car," Clara said, when she saw Robert put a key in the door of his 1988 green two-door Pontiac Fierro. He quickly helped Clara into the front seat, leaving me to squeeze into the back seat with Solow and my bulky purse. Robert crawled into the driver's seat and fired up the engine. From that moment on, throbbing engine noise took over and conversation became difficult.

A red light at the intersection temporarily brought the engine noise down to a rumble.

"Turn left, dear," Clara said to Robert. We made a left, cruised through town, past the Rec Center and over to San Lorenzo Avenue.

"Turn right," she prompted him.

"But aren't we going to our designated...?"

"Not right now, my dear. We have inside information and we'll search this area first," Clara said, in her sweet but unbending voice.

"Just follow those two horses up the hill," I said. But the horses began squirming and dancing because the Pontiac motor was so loud. Robert slowed the car when the girls turned their horses left onto a driveway leading to a small farm with a big barn.

"Turn, turn!" I shouted.

"Follow them," Clara ordered.

"Really?" Robert said.

"Really!" she said. "Those girls might know something."

Robert did as he was told, stopping the car near a large unpainted barn. The girls looked uneasy and so did the horses. Robert cut the engine and the horses settled down. We piled out of the car like four clowns from a circus car. It felt good to untangle my legs.

Grace leaned down from her horse and said, "Nice car," to Robert. His face reddened. "Nice barn," he stammered.

She dismounted, and let the sleek and muscled Arabian graze on new green grass lining the gravel driveway.

"The barn belongs to my friend's family. They have about five acres, five horses and lots of cats," Grace said, as her beautiful green eyes zoomed over Robert's wavy brown hair and landed on his blue eyes and goofy smile.

The sunny air felt warm and smelled like hay. I spotted two cats lounging on the front porch and two more stretched out on the hood of an older pickup truck.

Grace turned to follow her friend to the house.

"Just a minute, Grace," I said, "can I ask you a couple questions?"

"Sure, why not?"

"Are you joining the search?"

"Yeah, but my friend has to check in with her mom first."

"Do you know what you're looking for—what kind of clues?"

"We have a picture to show people," she said.

"That's great, but keep an eye out for jewelry. Remember the bracelet you gave me?"

Grace nodded.

"It turned out to be the real thing—rubies, emeralds and sapphires."

Her jaw dropped as her eyes widened. "No way!"

"It belonged to the murdered lady, Maria. Don't worry, I gave the bracelet to Alicia, Maria's sister…but then it turned up again." I watched Grace's friend walk toward us.

"What's your assignment?" Grace asked.

"We'll be taking a look at the upper end of San Lorenzo Avenue," I said.

"We do a lot of riding up there. Watch out for poison oak," Grace warned. "We'll be riding around the park all day, searching Bear Mountain in the morning and the river areas in the afternoon."

"Be careful along the river; it's really rushing with all the rain we've had."

Her friend came out of the house. Grace thanked me for the warning, turned and walked with her friend over to the horses. Each girl hooked a booted foot into a stirrup, lifted a long leg up and over the saddle and trotted down the driveway.

The girls were out of sight by the time we clowns crawled back into the Pontiac. Robert drove slowly, listening as Clara shouted instructions over motor noise. She'd decided we should drive up to the end of the road. The road dead-ended on the map, so we figured we'd work our way back down to Highway Nine hitting every house along the way.

"Nice plan, Auntie. I like to walk downhill."

A couple dozen sharp turns and two miles later we came to the end of the road. There were no signs, reflectors or anything. The pavement just ended and a narrow dirt road continued on around a turn.

Robert looped the Pontiac around and parked close to where the pavement ended.

Clara, Solow and I climbed out of the car.

"I love the smell of fireplace smoke. Don't you?" I said.

"I have plenty of that at home," Clara chuckled.

I finally realized that the forest was not a novelty to my aunt, it was "home."

But to me it was damp, dark and exciting. I sucked in the crisp air and imagined I heard wild animals. Solow was calm, so I knew there was no danger. I stood at the end of the blacktop looking at the damp earth, admiring three perfect pinecones still attached to a broken branch. How perfect nature was.

"Auntie, look!" I shouted.

"Tire tracks!" She bent down for a closer look. "Aren't these wider than regular car tracks?"

Robert slammed his door and stepped closer for a look. "You're right, Clara; the tracks are typical of trucks and vans. Actually, they look like the same size as the tires on my car."

Aunt Clara and I instantly turned and sized up Robert's wheels. Even though Robert was a very knowledgeable, responsible, hard-working, clean-cut guy—he was still young. His fancy rims and oversized tires expressed his youth perfectly.

Solow sniffed the tire tracks and began following them.

The three of us were close behind, silent and hopeful. Tramping over small broken branches lying in the mud, I realized that a vehicle had recently plowed through the foliage creating a tunnel for us to walk through. About a hundred feet in, the tunneling foliage and tracks swung to the right and stopped in front of a mossy old shack. Circling the one room excuse for a dwelling, we discovered it had two little windows, a door and nothing else except an outhouse a short distance away.

"Maybe it's a tool shed," Robert said.

"Out here all by itself?" Clara shook her head.

"It must be over a hundred years old," I estimated.

"Maybe an old prospector built it," Clara said, "and when his donkey died he decided he was tired of looking for gold and moved away."

Robert and I just rolled our eyes because laughing out loud had been suspended until happier times.

Walking up to the door, I tried the door knob. It turned but the door was stuck. I took a step back and then slammed my side against the warped wood. It gave.

Half expecting to see the old miner's ghost, I peeked around the musty room. "One rickety old bed and a bent-wood chair...wait a minute," I said, picking up an empty Cheetos bag off the floor. "Here's something for the red bag."

"Oh my!" Clara gulped, "The old miner was eating junk food!"

Robert started to laugh but suddenly we all knew the seriousness of the find.

Our eyes were on Solow as he sniffed the bag. Did he pick up a human scent or did he just love the smell of Cheetos? Finally, he left the bag, smelled the room thoroughly, then tramped out the door. We followed him as he headed to the outhouse and gave it the royal sniff. We followed Solow everywhere, examining every inch of the shack and the ground around it.

I took a few deep breaths and watched a yellow slug move slowly up the base of a young redwood tree. Nearby, a spider worked at mending its web. The forest was quiet. Where was Alicia? I opened my mouth, called her name as loud as I could and waited for an answer.

"It's going to be okay," Clara said, obviously hearing the anguish in my voice. She quickly wrapped her arms around me.

Robert walked back to his car.

I rested my head on Clara's shoulder and let out a few pent-up tears.

After a couple minutes, Clara said, "Let's get busy, dear. We'll go door to door and ask people if they've seen her."

"You're right, Auntie; we need to keep going," I sniffed.

We hustled down the muddy lane and stomped black clods from our shoes on the paved road before climbing into the nice clean Pontiac. The car obviously meant the world to Robert.

"Does someone have the Cheetos bag?" I asked.

"I put it in my red bag," Robert said, as we cruised a short distance down to the first house. A two-year-old in diapers answered the door. A minute later, a harried mother holding a newborn asked what was going on since few people made it all the way up to the end of the road.

Clara held up the eight by ten picture of Alicia. "Have you seen this woman?"

"She's very beautiful isn't she, but no, I haven't seen anyone. It's a joy to see you people up here. My husband works long hours and it gets lonely sometimes," she lamented.

"I'm sorry to hear that, my dear," Clara said. "Maybe you could join a young women's group, you know, where they have babysitters so that you can enjoy activities with your peers."

The young woman smiled. "Maybe when the baby's a little older. Thank you for the idea."

We shuffled down the street to the next house while Robert rolled the car slowly downhill. No one answered the door at the next two houses. We crossed the street and tried our luck at a friendly-looking red door. It opened and an elderly man peeked out.

"I'm not buying anything…" he grumped.

Clara held up the picture and asked if he'd seen her. Suddenly he had a twinkle in his eye and a smile on his wrinkly face. An old woman came up behind him and squeezed herself halfway out the door.

"Whatcha got there?" the woman asked.

"Have you seen this missing person?" I said.

"Isn't she the one who got killed over there at Roaring Camp?"

"No," Clara said, "this is the sister of the murdered woman. And you're right; they look very much alike."

The woman nodded. "Mac, put your tongue back in your mouth," she crabbed. "He used to have a reputation as a womanizer. Now he just dreams about it."

The next house we tried had a very long concrete driveway that curved and headed to the top of a knoll. Clara started huffing and puffing and dropped out. I kept walking until I came to a rather extravagant home. A woman walked out a second story door onto a balcony carrying a very large cat.

I craned my neck and said, "Hello; wonderful views up here."

"Hi, there; are you lost?"

"No, not lost. My name's Josephine and I'm looking for this woman—she's missing."

I held the picture up.

She put the cat down, leaned against the railing and said she'd never seen the woman before.

I thanked her and trotted back to the car. It wasn't our first rodeo and it wouldn't be our last.

My stomach growled.

Clara said she was hungry.

Robert was too.

"Okay, one more house and we'll get some lunch," I said.

The next house happened to be Howie's place. The green pickup was missing—a good sign, and so was Rory's puddle jumper. The only vehicle in the driveway was Dolly's Mini Cooper. We decided we would have a quick visit with Dolly before we went to town for food.

Dolly insisted we come inside. She said she was enjoying her day off by indulging in her favorite lunch—bologna sandwiches—and asked us to join her.

"My dear," Clara said, "we couldn't impose on you like that."

My stomach rumbled.

"You're hungry, aren't you?" Dolly said, looking at me and then Robert. He shrugged his shoulders and I nodded my head. I could see that she'd been making sandwiches for herself. She instantly went into mass production. When the platter of sandwiches was ready, she set the table and brought out a plate stacked with homemade lemon bars. We had a choice of hot tea or lemonade.

"Dolly, this lemon bar is amazing," Clara said. "By the way, are the men participating in the search for Alicia?"

"Rory went quail hunting." She rolled her eyes. "But Howie went out looking for Alicia at the crack of dawn."

When my plate was empty, I asked where the bathroom was.

"Around the corner, down the hall, second door on the right," Dolly giggled.

I walked through the kitchen and down the hall, past the second door and did a bit of snooping. At the end of the hall was a narrow staircase leading down to the first floor. I quietly padded down the stairs and stepped into Howie's bedroom. A section of built-in cabinets, the kind typically found in kitchens, lined one wall. One of the doors was wide open. To my surprise, Maria's picture from the *Sentinel* was taped to the door beside Alicia's picture from one of the flyers handed out. Did Howie have a crush on one or both of them? Why else would a grown man post a woman's picture?

On a hunch, I opened the opposite cupboard door. A picture of Howie, wearing a tux and standing next to a dark-haired girl dressed in a long gown, was taped to the cabinet door. It was obviously taken at a high school prom. The tape looked old and the kids looked young. I zeroed in on the girl because she reminded me of someone.

CHAPTER 19

After a fortifying lunch at Dolly's, Clara, Robert, Solow and I resumed our door-to-door search for Alicia. We concentrated on the lower half of San Lorenzo Avenue.

David called to report that there was not a single clue found in their designated search area.

"We found a couple things," I said. "I'll tell you about them when we meet at the Rec Center at four." We hung up. Just then a white van powered up the road. Instinctively, I glanced at the back plate. Blue, white and green; it was an Oregon plate.

"Did you see that?" I shouted. "That was the same kind of van that Del rented. Let's see where it goes."

"Okay, Josephine," Robert said, cranking the wheel and spinning the tires until we were headed up hill again. The old Pontiac growled as we gained speed.

"Step on it! We lost him," I shouted. Turn after turn I held my breath. When we reached the end of the road at the top of the hill, the van wasn't there. Robert turned the car around and we slowly headed back down hill, our eyes searching every driveway.

Suddenly, a white van entered the roadway in front of us on two wheels, coming from the red door property. It squealed, straightened and raced down the hill to the end of the road.

Robert sped up.

Without stopping, the van careened onto Highway Nine heading west.

Seconds later, Robert's Green Pontiac Fierro was heading west. His car handled the tight turns fairly well. Highway Nine had no straight sections, only miles and miles of sharp turns, as it mimicked the course of the San Lorenzo River and a set of narrow gauge railroad tracks.

Aunt Clara looked pale. One hand lay over her chest and the other was fisted around a loop hanging from the ceiling for that purpose.

I didn't feel very well due to my full tummy swaying side to side in the back seat, but my adrenaline was pumping. Even Solow felt the excitement and howled at the window. Crazy thoughts crossed my mind, like, who built that railroad and how did they do it? High above the river, the railroad trestles leaped from one piece of protruding land to another.

"Should I be worried about a train coming?" Robert asked.

"No, they hardly ever do a run into Santa Cruz," I assured him.

"I think I hear a train," Clara said.

"Are you kidding?" he laughed a cynical laugh.

"Really, I hear it…" Clara sputtered.

"Holy you know what!" Robert yelled as he braked and swerved just in time for the train to angle across Highway Nine in front of us. "That was close!" He wiped his forehead with a shaky hand. "Must be a dry run. All the cars were empty."

The Pontiac engine had stalled from the quick stop. Robert tried the ignition a few times, flooding the engine. Finally it kicked over and we continued on our way.

"I don't know if I can catch up to the van," Robert said.

"There's no place to turn around," I told him; "we might as well drive the rest of the way into Santa Cruz. I have a theory. There's a pretty good chance the van driver doesn't really want to go to Santa Cruz. All he wanted to do was out-run us. Why don't we go back to the Felton neighborhood and wait for him?"

"I think that makes sense," Clara nodded her head. "We're almost to Fern Street. Robert, dear, just turn right on Fern, whup it around the block and come out on Coral."

Always respectful to his elders, Robert skillfully did as he was told.

With no time to lose, we needed to be waiting somewhere along San Lorenzo Avenue. *How does one hide a classic avocado green Pontiac?* I wondered. Minutes ticked by as we wove a curvy path through the forest, bouncing around the car's interior like golden kernels in a popcorn machine. My left shoulder felt like it did years ago when I'd miscalculated the distance between two trees while skiing downhill. Every turn in the two-lane highway jerked me against the metal door frame. Sometimes I forgot to brace and the side of my head would hit the window.

"What's that thunking noise back there?" Clara asked.

"Don't worry, Auntie; it's me and the door getting to know each other."

Solow looked at me with sad eyes. Then his belly rumbled and he got the dry heaves going. I talked to him, consoled him and pushed him away from me. I started feeling like I wanted to let go of my lunch too. Just when I thought neither of us could hold it much longer, the old Pontiac swung left up San Lorenzo Avenue. I asked Robert to park in Howie's driveway.

"Just back it in," Clara instructed, as if she knew how to drive.

Robert over-shot the driveway, then backed the car into it on command.

"Way back!" I said.

He stopped the car inches behind Dolly's Mini Cooper.

I opened my door and pulled Solow out. He dry heaved again.

"I'll be right back," I said, as I hooked Solow to his leash, ran up the long staircase and banged on the front door.

Dolly appeared looking frightened. "Oh, it's you!" She started to smile.

"Can you take Solow for a little while? We think we know where Alicia might be," I said, breathlessly.

Dolly's mouth gaped as she took the end of the leash I handed her.

"Thanks, Dolly!" I yelled over my shoulder, already pounding down the stairs. Feeling revived from the fresh air, I squeezed myself in behind Robert's seat and buckled up.

"Too bad you only have two doors," I grumped.

"How many doors do you have, Josephine?" he asked.

"Just two...look! There goes the van!" I shouted.

Robert drove to the end of the driveway, stopped and we all looked up the road to our right.

The van disappeared around a turn.

We motored up the road slowly, looking up every driveway.

"Robert, can I take a look at the Cheetos bag?"

"Ah, sure. Can you get it out of the glove box?" he asked Clara.

Aunt Clara found the red bag, pulled the Cheetos bag out of it and peeked inside. "Oh, there's something in it. Is this what you're looking for?" she asked, handing over a tiny scrap of paper not much bigger than a postage stamp.

"Thank you, Auntie. Alicia keeps putting things out for us to find and this looks like a time and place for something important. It reads, "end of wharf #2, T 15 7:15. Someone catching a boat ride?"

My mind suddenly went blank. "What's today? What's the date?"

"Oh my, today's the fifteenth of November," Clara gulped, "and maybe the *T* stands for Tuesday. I think it means today, tonight actually, at seven-fifteen. It couldn't be seven-fifteen in the morning because we just saw Mr. Block in the van this afternoon. Obviously he hasn't caught the boat yet," she smiled wickedly.

"Robert, you can drop us at the Rec Center," I said.

"Oh, no you don't, Josephine! Alicia's my friend too and I'm gonna find her."

"So where are we going?" I asked him.

He was quick to answer. "The only wharf number two that I know about is the one in Monterey." His car rumbled through Felton, up and over Graham Hill Road and eventually entered Highway One where we experienced the usual fishhook slow-down.

"Something important will happen at seven-fifteen at the end of the wharf," I predicted. "End of the wharf must mean there's a boat involved. Leaving after dark? I didn't know that boats left in the dark."

"We need to find Alicia before that happens." Clara groaned.

I pulled out my phone and called Alicia's house phone. It rang many times and finally Ernie's recorded voice asked me to leave a message. "Del, if you can hear me, it's Josephine. Please answer the phone. It's very important that I talk to you!" I shouted. I hung up and dialed the number again, ready to leave another message. Del came on the line and said something in a weak congested voice.

"Del, thank goodness you answered. We think we might be on the trail to finding Alicia. Tell me how to get to your island and the name of it?"

"Josephine, it is funny you ask. Last night I remembered the name. It is the island of Guadalupe." He took a moment to cough. "Excuse me, por favor. To get to the island you must find an excursion boat, one that searches for great white sharks. The only other boats that go to the island belong to Enrique and his friends."

Chills ran up and down my spine at the thought of sharks of any kind, and even more shivers when I thought about Enrique and his men.

Del blew his nose and returned to the phone. "I think Iggy Vargas is the persona you will be dealing with. Be very careful, he is an expert in martial arts. He will do anything to make Enrique happy. I suspect he wants to offer Alicia to Enrique in place of Maria. You must not let that happen," Del coughed and sputtered.

He had just confirmed my worst fears.

"What does Iggy look like?" I already had a pretty good idea, but thought I'd ask Del while I had him on the phone.

"He is big and very fit, with short black hair and a scar on his cheek."

"Okay, thanks Del. You sound terrible. Go back to bed."

We hung up.

"Robert, your car doesn't have a clock on the dash," I grumped.

"Does yours?"

"No, but I wear a watch and it's now five-forty. We have less than two hours to get to Monterey and make a plan."

"Are you kidding? A plan?" Robert said, as he drove into his mother's Watsonville neighborhood. "You want a plan? I have a plan. We'll stop at my apartment and I'll get my Mom's gun."

"What? Now who's kidding?" I yelled from the back seat.

"Not kidding! Are you going to take on this black-belt guy, Josephine?"

"His name is Iggy Vargas," I snapped.

"Don't look at me," Clara said.

The stars were coming out and a full moon peeked over the eastern hills. It was a beautiful night but none of us would remember the fair weather and iridescent moon. Our thoughts were on Alicia. What condition was she in after being dragged around by that ruffian?

"Robert, is your mom home?"

"Nope, she works the late shift," he said, as the Pontiac sidled up to the curb and he cut the engine. "I'll be right back." He leaped out of the car and ran up the sidewalk.

A few minutes later, Robert was back with a big lump in his jacket. He tried to sit down but the lump was in the way. He pulled the gun out of his waistband and shoved it under the driver's seat.

"That thing looks like a cowboy six-shooter. Did you bring bullets?" Clara asked.

"Just one in the chamber," he said, firing up the Pontiac. "I didn't have time to look for more. It's already after six." He made a tight turn in the road and we took off for Monterey. "By the way, which wharf is number two wharf?"

Clara looked over her shoulder at me.

I shrugged. "We'll have to ask around."

Fortunately, traffic wasn't too bad on the last stretch of the highway heading south.

Clara's head dropped back, her gentle snores absorbed by classic-car engine noise.

I pulled Dolly's card out of my purse and punched in her number.

"Hello?"

"Hi, Dolly; this is Josephine. Is everything okay? I mean is Solow behaving?"

"He threw up in my kitchen. How long did you say…"

"I didn't really say how long it would take, but we're arriving in Monterey right now. We have reason to believe Alicia is going to be put on a boat at wharf number two. Is that the narrow wharf or the one with all the restaurants?"

"Oh my, I think it's the long narrow one but I could be wrong," she said. "I guess I won't see you for a while."

"We don't know how this will play out. Keep your fingers crossed and don't feed Solow anything greasy. Thanks a lot!" I hung up quickly when I noticed that my battery was on its last leg. I dropped the phone into my purse just as Robert exited Del Monte Boulevard.

"Robert, not this wharf!" I shouted, glancing at my watch.

"I'm going to park over here because people tend to recognize my car."

"You're right about that," Clara said, rubbing and blinking her eyes.

Robert finally settled on a place to park next to three giant dumpsters. He tucked the gun back into his waist band, zipped up his jacket and held the seat back for me, making it easier for me to crawl out. It felt good to stand but my legs trembled. Was it an earthquake or nerves? Robert had already started walking fast toward wharf number two. All I had to do was catch up to him and save Alicia.

"Stay in the car and keep warm!" I shouted to Clara over my shoulder.

"It's seven o'clock, dear; be safe!" she yelled at my back as I hurried to catch up to Robert.

As desperately urgent as the situation was, my senses were on steroids. I smelled the salty air, heard gulls in the distance, saw the moon rising over choppy water and felt cold off-shore breezes as they ruffled my hair. I wondered what Alicia was doing at that moment as I loped across two blocks of half empty parking lot. Near the entrance to wharf number two, I caught up to Robert. We looked at each other and suddenly realized we were scared silly.

"If you see a white van, just turn your back so they don't know it's you," Robert advised.

"You have a hood on your jacket," I said, lifting the thing up over his head. "Iggy Vargas doesn't even know you. Robert, I think you should go first and I'll be ready to hide behind you. I wish these street lights weren't on. Actually, they make you look orange," I laughed nervously.

Two restaurants at the beginning of the wharf were doing a good business. Once we passed the laughing, talking customers, we became noticeable as the only two people walking to the end of the pier. Wharf number two was about two blocks long with wooden railings on each side and a couple of warehouses near the end.

Water lapped against the wharf's pilings giving the structure and my confidence a little shake with each wave. The ocean sights and sounds were usually a comfort to me, but not on this dreaded Tuesday night.

"Slow down," I whispered to Robert. "I can't keep up with you. Besides, it's only ten after seven." He slowed a bit, but I knew he was wound tighter than my Timex. Suddenly, a pair of headlights killed all the safety shadows I'd planned to dive into.

A white van rolled by.

Robert stopped abruptly but my feet kept going, right up the back of his heels. We separated and then casually meandered over to the left railing to stare at the water. We were about ten yards from the end of the wharf where ominous headlights pointed out a break in the railing and steps leading down to the water.

A large fishing boat, silhouetted by the moon, moved with the rhythm of a stormy sea.

CHAPTER 20

Surging forward in the dark, I thought of my courageous friend Alicia. As I sprinted toward the end of wharf number two, Robert tried to pull me back. My coattail slipped out of his hand.

A cloud suddenly wiped out the moon.

I had to bring it down to a slow walk because I couldn't see the uneven planks under my feet. Up ahead I did see one small light atop an antenna that stretched upward from the cabin of an unusually large fishing boat spewing exhaust into the pristine ocean air.

A blockish silhouette stepped out of the white van and took a couple steps down the stairs.

"Wait!" I shouted.

The block stopped and turned his head.

"Where's Alicia?" I didn't need to shout. I'd caught up to him and was close enough to smell Cheetos on his breath, but a shout came out anyway.

Robert came up behind me.

"Your lady friend no want to go. She run away two nights ago," he bellowed. Enrique will kill me, maybe."

Finally, Robert was able to free his gun from his waistband. He pointed the muzzle at Iggy.

"Little muchachos should not play with guns," the block snorted.

"Give us Alicia or I'll blow your head off!"

"Robert, I don't think she's…"

"Bang!"

Iggy laughed as the antenna light exploded into a zillion pieces. It might have been a nervous laugh, because he quickly jumped aboard. In seconds, the boat had moved away from the wharf and turned out to sea.

Tears streamed down my face. It was the end of the world. All hope was gone.

"Come on, Jo; let's take a look in the van."

I stood paralyzed as dark dread held me in its fist.

"I'll take a look," Robert said, as he walked a few feet to the vehicle.

After a thorough search, he said, "Let's get out of here." He gave my shoulder an awkward pat. The wharf seemed ten miles long. As we passed the restaurants, I wondered why people were still going about the business of eating and enjoying life. Robert hooked his arm into mine. We continued our walk through the extensive but practically empty parking lot. I almost smiled in the dark thinking about how brave he was, and what a bad shot.

"I know how disappointed you must be," Robert said, as if he could read my mind.

Stopping on a dime, I asked him, "What would you have done if you'd actually shot Iggy Vargas?"

"Someone would write a song entitled, 'The Man who Shot Iggy Vargas.'" he laughed. "It was just a threat, Jo. Actually, I was aiming for the boat. I wanted to put a hole in it so it wouldn't float."

"That was a noble idea, my friend, but your shot was about twenty-five feet too high."

"Yeah, this gun has quite a kick."

"Now to tell Clara we failed. Oh my gosh. I need to tell David and Ernie and Del and I have to tell Dolly when we go back to pick up Solow."

"Don't worry, I'll help you tell them," Robert offered. "The problem I see is that Iggy obviously doesn't have Alicia. So who does? If she ran away like he said, she's probably in the Felton area. I wonder why she hasn't called for help."

"In the beginning she was probably held in the shack up at the end of San Lorenzo Avenue because that's where we found the Cheetos bag," I said, "and Cheetos never lie."

"You mean Cheetos never prosper," Robert corrected me.

We came close to laughing, but not quite.

Robert opened the car door and pulled the seat forward for me.

Clara seemed to be holding her breath as she waited to hear what had happened, since Alicia obviously wasn't with us.

As I crawled into the back seat, Clara made small talk about the lovely moon reflected on Monterey Bay. I could barely stand hearing her sappy words. What I needed was another good cry but I had no more tears. I felt empty and useless. It was time to go home and face all the people I'd let down.

Robert slid into his seat. "Anyone hungry for dinner?"

Clara said she was starving.

"Since we're already parked near wharf number one, why don't we go down there for some clam chowder or something?" Robert suggested.

"Yeah, I really want to eat a dead fish," I said to myself. But the consensus was that we should have dinner at the wharf since Monterey had very few fast food establishments, if any. Robert held the seat back for me, sensing my ugly mood. He kept quiet as the three of us walked a block over to the wharf and out to a restaurant near the end.

Once Robert was comfortably waiting for his clam chowder in a bread bowl, he began to talk about our encounter with Iggy. He told my aunt how far we had to walk and described the fishing boat. As he talked, I realized that the long walk to the end of the pier might be considered an athletic experience in his world.

Clara sat up straight in her chair, wide-eyed, as Robert described his shoot-out with Iggy Vargas.

"My, my, Robert, aren't you the daring one!" she cooed, and then looked at me. "I'm so sorry you didn't find Alicia, my dear." Her words worked as a temporary bandage over my heart. "Don't forget to eat your salad."

I gave her a "mind your own business look," and instantly regretted it.

Clara sipped her soup and engaged Robert in small talk, enabling me to stay in my own little self-pity cocoon until I was ready to reenter the world. My aunt knew me pretty well. And I knew her moods too—always patient, always kind. I wanted to live up to her example, but so far it had been impossible.

Robert tore off a piece of soggy sourdough bread, "The good thing is, Alicia isn't headed for an island off the coast of Mexico." He popped the bread into his mouth.

"Do you want my calamari?" I asked the starving young grocery clerk.

"I'll take the big piece, but you better finish eating the other one," he said, obviously concerned I might lose weight and become a stick-figure. Not in a million years!

I picked up my plate with one hand and gave the calamari steak a shove with my knife. It flew onto Robert's plate and was quickly devoured. Our waitress circled the table, took away Clara's empty plate and circled again. Knowing how late it was on a Tuesday night, I quickly paid the bill so we could go home. As soon as Robert swallowed his last bite, we traipsed outside into the dark night. A blustery wind at our backs pushed us toward the Pontiac. I peeked into the classic car wishing Alicia would be sitting there waiting to go home.

Once we were buckled up, Robert suggested I call David and Ernie to let them know where we were. It was a good idea except that my phone had been dead for a couple hours and the Pontiac was way too old to have a cell phone charger. Robert said he'd left his phone in his other jacket and Aunt Clara didn't own a cell phone.

"Jo, there's one thing I don't understand," Robert said. "You told me your ranger friend was beaten up. Do you think Iggy did it? If he did, why?"

"I think the guy did it because Dolly and Howie picked him out of a police line-up," I said, "but I'm just speculating."

"I knew I should have shot him!" he snarked.

It was ten o'clock when we finally rolled into Felton. I could tell that Robert was tired. He'd quit talking, or maybe I quit hearing him because I fell asleep in the back seat. He dropped Clara and me at the Rec Center and waited a few minutes to make sure my truck started.

He tooted his horn once and drove away.

Clara and I buckled up, shivering like two Chihuahuas in a snowstorm until the heater began to put out some warmth. Quietly, we rode a short distance on Highway Nine, turned up San Lorenzo Avenue and crunched up the familiar driveway. Clara said she needed to move around and get her blood circulating, so she followed me up the stairs to Dolly's door. I was glad to see lights coming from almost every window, upstairs and down.

I knocked on the door.

Dolly opened it wearing fuzzy baby blue pajamas.

Solow stood at her side.

I reached down for a quick cuddle with my buddy.

"Solow was a good boy," Dolly said, pushing a glob of fuzzy grey hair back from her face. Without the bonnet she looked like an average sixty-year-old woman.

"Sorry we're so late," I said.

"My, it's late, isn't it? I haven't been up this late in years," Dolly chuckled. "It's kind of exciting. How did it go?"

Clara stepped inside. "Our friend shot a boat, but that was all."

I followed my aunt into the house. "We had a tip, but it turned out Alicia wasn't there," I explained.

"You girls need a cuppa hot tea. Sit down over there and I'll get some."

"You are so sweet," Clara said, as Dolly disappeared into the kitchen. "Where's her husband?" she whispered to me.

I shrugged my shoulders. "His car wasn't in the driveway."

Dolly poked her head around the corner. "What do you like in your tea?"

"Just tea," Clara said.

"Same for me," I said, not wishing to stay very long.

"Did you hear that?" I whispered to Clara.

She nodded. "Sounded like somebody dropped something heavy."

Must be Howie downstairs, I thought to myself.

Dolly came back with the tea.

"Would you mind if I used your phone?" I said.

"Oh my, of course, you may. We gave up the land line," she giggled, as she pulled a shiny new cell phone from her baggy pajama pants pocket and handed it to me.

Letting the tea cool, I began making the dreaded phone calls. David had already gone to bed but he was used to my irregular habits and exploits. Remembering his soothing words helped me to get through the calls to Ernie and Ben. When I finally got to Ben's call, Clara was sound asleep.

"Hold on, Ben. Dolly's asking me something."

"Why don't you two sleep here on my couches?" she said.

"Ben, we've been invited to stay at Dolly's house in Felton tonight."

"Okay, see you tomorrow." Ben hadn't sounded surprised when I told him that Clara had already crashed on the couch. He said he was relieved to hear from us and know we were okay.

Dolly disappeared down the hall and a minute later came back with a stack of folded blankets. She held them out to me. I took two from the top, spread one heavy blanket over Clara and tucked her in. I spread a fuzzy blanket over the other couch and wrapped myself in it.

Dolly set the extra blankets on the coffee table, excused herself and turned off the lights on her way to bed.

Solow continued his slumber, lying at the foot of my couch. Trying to get comfortable, I tried various throw pillows, sometimes two or three at a time. My mind kept recreating the boat-shooting scene over and over. Finally, I put one of the pillows over my head and hummed the *Star Spangled Banner* softly.

Solow and Aunt Clara slept while I wondered where Alicia was. Finally I sat up. *Might as well look around,* I thought to myself, as I slowly tip-toed down the hall. Not a noise anywhere, except for a tapping sound coming from a room downstairs. Out of curiosity, I crept down the stairs. As I neared the bottom step, I saw a sliver of light under Howie's door.

I finally realized the tapping had stopped.

I froze, eyes wide.

Out of the dark end of the little hallway to my left, Howard suddenly appeared. "Oh, it's you, Josephine," he said. "Why are you here?"

216

"My aunt and I are spending the night here and I couldn't sleep."

"I couldn't sleep either," Howard said, opening his bedroom door. "Do you want to come in and sit down?"

"Oh, no, not really. I'm just out for the exercise. By the way, your bruises are looking better—almost gone. How are you feeling?"

"I'm good. Would you like to see the leather belt I'm making?"

"Not right now, Howie, but I'm curious. Can you tell me who beat you up?"

"Sure. It was Iggy Vargas. I thought everybody knew that."

"Not everyone knows that. Why did he do it?"

"Because Mom and I picked him out in the line-up," he said matter-of-factly.

"Why did you pick him out? What did he do wrong?"

"That night on the train, Iggy was the one who tried to pull Maria away from her brother. I saw the whole thing. She stood up to get away. He came at her, and she stepped up onto the bench seat. She pulled back to get away from him and lost her balance. Maria's brother leaned over the side of the car, trying to pull her back into the train. Iggy grabbed the brother's pant leg, but it was too late. He went over the side with Maria. He landed beside the tracks, but she went over the side of the trestle." Howard slumped against the wall. "I have nightmares about it every night."

"But you told me you didn't ride the train."

"I know and I'm sorry, Josephine. I wasn't ready to talk about what I saw. It was a terrible thing!"

"I'm sorry you had to suffer through this. Do you have any idea where Alicia is?" I begged. "I'm really scared for her safety."

"I wish I knew. That's one more reason I can't sleep." He looked ready to cry.

"Okay, well, I'm going back upstairs. Hope you can get some rest."

I laid back on the couch, the night was very quiet until a vehicle crunched up the gravel driveway. Headlights lit up the living room and a second later everything went dark. A car door slammed. Heavy footsteps thunder half-way up the front stairs, paused and then pounded back down the steps.

Someone knocked on a door downstairs.

I heard muffled voices. Male voices.

A door slammed.

Another door slammed.

Sleep was out of the question so I tiptoed to the front window and looked down at moonlight reflecting off the roof of my truck. Next to it was Rory's puddle-jumper. It was Rory who'd finally come home, but had decided to stay downstairs.

Back on the couch, I curled up and fell asleep a little after two o'clock.

Later, I woke up with a start and tried to remember where I was. Dolly's tea came to mind. From there I was able to piece together an evening I'd wished I could forget. Looking around in the dark, I asked myself why I woke up. My lazy brain finally let me remember the sound of glass breaking. Instead of worrying about the noise, I fell back on my stack of pillows and passed out.

The next time I opened my eyes the living room was flooded with light.

Aunt Clara bustled around the room straightening pillows and folding blankets.

"Good morning, dear," she smiled.

"Morning."

"Dolly has already gone to work. Such a busy girl," Clara laughed.

"Is anyone else up?"

"I haven't seen anyone. Dolly left us half a pot of coffee. Would you like a cup?"

"Sure, why not?" I crabbed, then apologized for sounding like a beast.

"Ben will make us a lovely breakfast, and then you'll feel better," she said.

I folded my blanket, proceeded down the hall to the linen closet and shoved the blanket into a small space at the top of the stack. I closed the door and continued down the hall to the narrow staircase. No one was around. I crept slowly down the steps, stopping to listen every couple steps. As I drew closer to the bedroom area, I heard snoring—not gentle snoring like Aunt Clara produced. It sounded like it came from a giant ape suffering from a bad cold.

I knew that the bedroom on the left belonged to Howie, but the heaviest snores came from the bedroom on the right.

Suddenly the loudest snore stopped while the gentler snoring continued.

I whirled around and skittered up the stairs. My heart was pounding as I slowed my walk to a casual stroll and entered the kitchen.

"What pink cheeks you have, my dear," Clara said, touching my forehead with her fingers. "No fever," she concluded.

"I was exploring the two bedrooms downstairs. Howie and Rory are still asleep. Rory got home really late last night."

"Is that a bad thing?" Rory said, as he entered the kitchen, scratching his bare belly above his sweat pants. "I get home late six days a week because I work the late shift at Orly's Barbecue Bunker and Bar in Boulder Creek."

Clara nodded. "You poor thing, working those unnatural hours."

Solow wandered into the kitchen and smelled Rory's bare feet.

The man poured himself a mug of coffee. "So what are you two doing here? It's fine with me, you understand. I have great respect for women." He smiled, "and I really like dogs."

"But you don't have one," I said.

"Yeah, right, so what are you gals doing here?"

"We arrived pretty late last night to pick up Solow, and Dolly invited us to stay the night," I said, watching the man pull a half-eaten donut from the pantry, bite into it and brush the crumbs off his hairy chest onto the floor.

"Well, ladies, off I go to unplug a stupid toilet downstairs." He rounded the corner, thunked his bare feet to the end of the hall and down the stairs. I figured Rory could always find his way back to the kitchen—just follow the donut crumbs.

Clara and I wolfed our coffee down, rinsed the cups and quickly left Dolly's home. Solow seemed happy to be leaving as he snuggled up with Clara's feet under the dash.

Heading north on Highway Nine, we finally entered Big Basin Highway. Thankful for daylight and dry conditions, I drove up Clara and Ben's long driveway. As we approached the house, the first thing I noticed was the freshly cut rounds of redwood and a new window replacement.

Solow woke up suddenly and howled. It was a howl he used expressly for just two things—Fluffy and bacon, and Fluffy wasn't around.

"It was sweet of Dolly to let us stay the night," Clara said, "but I'm so happy to be home." She quickly climbed out of the truck, helped Solow to the ground and stretched out her arms. The view was breath-taking from the top of the hill. As Clara opened the back door, a heavenly bacon smell engulfed us. My stomach growled. I hadn't had much of an appetite for food the night before.

"I hope I don't hurt Ben's feelings, but I'm not very hungry."

"Dear, you don't have to eat very much, just sit with us for a little while. Ben is always happy to see you."

A few minutes later, we sat down on Clara's lovely antique chairs at the big country table. Ben said he had something to show us. He held a little yellow piece of fabric in the palm of his hand for us to see.

"Where did that come from?" I gasped.

"I found it stuck in a manzanita branch at the top of San Lorenzo Avenue yesterday. I didn't turn it in to the police because I wanted to check with you first, Josephine. I thought you might know..."

CHAPTER 21

It was a Wednesday morning like no other, sitting at Clara and Ben's table having a beautiful breakfast and not tasting a thing. My heart raced when I first saw the little piece of yellow cloth in Ben's hand. It was exactly the same in color and texture as Alicia's jacket. I was sure she'd set it out for someone to discover.

"Was there anything else with it?" Clara asked. Ben shook his head, no.

I had questions, but I was unable to put two words together even though my mouth was obviously open.

"Just the cloth with a little branch poked into it…" Ben said, "probably put there on purpose."

"Near the shack?" I could barely breathe.

"Not exactly; you see Ernie and I hiked around the shack and found this little deer trail behind the outhouse."

"Where was David?" I asked.

"His ankle was acting up so he put on the boot and stayed on the paved road. He told us later he'd visited a few houses and showed some people Alicia's picture."

"We covered the shack area already, but it never hurts to be thorough," Clara said, as she passed a plate of hash browns my way.

I added a big scoop of potatoes to my plate of scrambled eggs and bacon because I was finally able to enjoy the food. Mentally, I had a plan—a place to start. Silently, I plotted and planned to go to the shack, find the deer trail and walk it with Solow. Ben and Clara were too old. They'd slow me down. If I told them what I wanted to do they might try to stop me.

"I thought you weren't hungry, Josephine?" Clara teased, as food quickly disappeared from my plate.

"Don't worry; that little yellow scrap has set my appetite on fire. Please pass the butter." As my tummy filled, I began covertly stuffing the paper napkin on my lap with toast and bacon.

"I'm glad you're enjoying the food." Ben raised an eyebrow and smiled.

"You're a wonderful cook," I said, secretly adding another piece of bacon to my stash.

They talked, but I had no idea what they said because my mind was back in Felton imagining a reunion with Alicia. I hurried through my breakfast, slipped one more piece of bacon and another piece of toast onto the paper napkin on my lap. I excused myself from the table.

"Is there anything we can do for you, Josephine, before you leave?" Ben asked.

"Do you have a bottle of water I can take with me?"

He pulled a bottle out of the fridge.

While his back was turned, I shoved the wadded napkin full of food into my jacket pocket.

"Okay, Solow, time to go."

Sara jumped up and looked at me like she was ready to go for a ride. She thunked her ninety-pound body down on the kitchen floor when she realized we were leaving her behind.

Even though Aunt Clara knew me inside and out, it was Ben who looked into my blood-shot eyes and knew I'd never stop looking for my friend. Ben handed me the yellow fabric and wished me luck.

"Thank you for everything, Ben," I said, as Solow snatched a last bite of Sara's kibble and followed me out the door.

Right behind us, Clara and Ben stood watching. "We're wishing you luck, Josephine," Ben said, and raised a thumb.

Clara blew kisses as we drove away.

Back on the road again, my high hopes for finding Alicia were periodically attacked by imaginary monsters named Fear and Dread. Ms. Fear was afraid I wouldn't find my friend, and Ms. Dread was afraid I would find her, but not in time.

It was close to ten o'clock when Solow and I cruised through Felton. The sun was out and the town was buzzing with cars and people. As we came closer to the Rec Center, my buddy pressed his nose to the window. The Center's parking lot was full of people and parked cars. Vehicles lined both sides of the road for several blocks. The search party turnout was amazing and heartwarming.

Clusters of jay-walkers skittered across the street, joining their friends who were studying maps and receiving instruction from police officers. Each day the number of volunteers had increased. I felt like smiling but couldn't quite do it.

A minute later, the crowd was behind us. Ahead loomed San Lorenzo Avenue and a shack at the top of the hill. Solow howled when Grace and her friend passed by us riding their horses downhill.

"Sometimes I think you'd rather be with them," I told Solow, "but I'm going to need that famous nose of yours. I wish I had something bigger than this little piece of Alicia's jacket for you to smell."

At the top of the hill, the paved road ended but we kept going. The muddy extension leading to the shack had dried out, making it easier to park near the little building. According to radio news, no rain was expected for the next three days. When I heard the prediction, I took it with a grain of salt.

I heard a car coming closer and looked in my rearview mirror.

"That's weird. That looks like Dolly's car."

Solow yawned.

I climbed down from my seat, rounded the truck and helped Solow to the ground. By that time, Dolly was waving and shouting something.

"Hi, Dolly, what did you ask me?"

"Are you going to look for Alicia?"

"Actually...yeah. Solow and I are going..."

"Can I come with you?" Her plump little body shook with excitement.

"I'll be doing a lot of uphill climbing."

"I can do that. I want to help," she pleaded.

I had to admit she looked more fit in blue jeans and a sweatshirt than in her usual flouncy dress and bonnet.

"Josephine, I went to work this morning but I couldn't stay, knowing Alicia was out there somewhere. I went home, changed my clothes and reported in at the Rec Center. That's when I saw you drive by."

"Well, I guess it'd be nice to have company."

Dolly ran back to her Mini Cooper, grabbed her heavy jacket, locked the door and dropped the car key into her pocket.

Solow was already sniffing the turf at the back of the shack. I found the deer trail I'd seen previously and showed it to Dolly thinking she might not like the looks of it and would un-invite herself. After all, she was sixty if she was a day.

"Good thing I'm short," she giggled.

We went down on our knees and crawled about thirty feet through a tunnel carved out of small tree branches, wild lilac bushes and prickly weeds. At the end of the deer trail, we stood up and walked across a meadow ringed in oaks and manzanita. New green grass covered several acres, sprinkled with ceanothus and poison oak in its winter form.

"Watch out for those long leafless spiky things," I warned Dolly; "it's poison oak."

Dolly said she was a third-generation Californian and knew what poison oak looked like in all its forms. She charged ahead with amazing energy. In fact, I struggled to keep up with her. Solow led the way, nose to the ground except whenever a squirrel crossed his path.

Pleasant weather had us shedding jackets and sweating buckets. The sun's position told us it was noon. I checked my watch. The sun was right on time.

The terrain got steeper.

My tummy growled. I decided I'd call out Alicia's name every time my stomach growled instead of thinking about food. I called her name over and over in the beginning.

Dolly was silent.

"Are you okay, Dolly?" I asked as we crested our first little mountain.

"Yes, I'm fine, Josephine...how are you doing?"

"When we get to the bottom of this hill, let's take a break," I suggested.

"That would be lovely," she said, half loping, half rolling down the mulchy western slope. We zig-zagged down the mountain, dodging brambles, logs and ruts. At the bottom, I leaped over a narrow rushing brook. Dolly jumped onto a large rock before leaping the rest of the way across. From there we climbed uphill over rocks and dead branches until we found a small hillside clearing graced with dappled sunshine and a view of the stream below.

Dolly plopped down on the soft leafy earth.

Solow and I dropped down beside her, still trying to catch a breath.

"Where did you learn to climb like that, Dolly?"

"Growing up, I had two big brothers to keep up with," she laughed, "and their legs were long!"

"How's Howie doing? Is he fully recovered?" I asked.

"He's better, but I think my poor boy's still a bit traumatized by the October event. Seeing that poor woman fall out of the train had to be tough. He has a hard time sleeping." Slap! Dolly smacked an ugly bug trying to crawl up her ankle. "He didn't even tell me about it until a couple days ago." She pulled a Kleenex out of her pocket and cleaned bug remains off her hand and leg.

"Now that you know Howie was on the train and saw what happened that night, would it make a difference if you were asked again to pick someone from a lineup?"

"Not really," Dolly swatted gnats away from her face. "Because the cops just wanted to know if Mr. Vargas was at the park on Halloween night. He was, and we both saw him. I feel we did the right thing. So far he hasn't been accused of murder. But now that he's gone, I guess he'll never have to pay the price for what he did."

"I don't think it was murder, just an attempted kidnapping that went south. I talked to Howie last night," I said, swatting at little flying gnats buzzing around my ear, "but I'm wondering about your take on what happened."

"Howie told me it was a terrible accident," Dolly sighed. "This horrible Iggy person tried to grab the woman, Maria. He frightened her, so she stood up on her seat. He reached toward her and she leaned back, away from him. It was all very sad. And then the gentleman sitting next to her tried to pull Maria back into the car and ended up falling out of the train too. I wonder what happened to him."

"Actually, Clara and I found him lying alongside Highway Nine near your neighborhood. We took him to my house and he's doing okay. At first we didn't even know he was Maria's brother."

"But you took him home with you anyway...my, my."

"His name is Del. He had a gash on his forehead and lost his memory, but his recall is coming back piece by piece. I can't wait to hear him talk about what happened Halloween night. I'd like to know how—a day later—he ended up almost a mile away on Highway Nine."

Dolly stood up, brushed dead leaves off her rump and suggested we start up the mountain. I fell in behind her as she struggled to keep up with Solow. We were headed in a north-westerly direction, according to the sun's position, when we heard the whap, whap rumble of a faraway helicopter. My heart beat double time. I was cautiously encouraged, but it was impossible for us to see very much sky through the thick canopy created by hundreds of redwoods.

After another two hours of steep climbing and calling Alicia's name, we topped our second mountain range and descended the western side. Again, we crossed a stream at the bottom and collapsed on the other side—the cold shady side.

Dolly scrunched down on her belly and reached into the cold clear water. A few slurps and she was satisfied. "Don't worry, Josephine; it's clean."

I went down on my knees, leaned forward and scooped cold water with my hands. It looked and tasted clean and delicious. I sat back and pulled out a bulging napkin from my pocket. I opened it and offered Dolly what looked like croutons and bacon chips.

"Nice of you to pack a lunch," Dolly giggled.

"It was part of my breakfast. Who knows when we'll eat again. Dolly, I have a confession to make."

She looked at me. "You can tell me...we're friends, aren't we?"

"Yes we are," I said. "I was sort of looking around in Howie's room and I saw a picture of Maria and one of Alicia posted on the inside of a cupboard door."

After an uncomfortably pregnant silence, Dolly told me the pictures were Howie's pin-ups. He had a crush on both of the women, but it didn't mean he'd done anything wrong.

Deep shadows fell across our forest way-station, as Mr. Sun favored the western slopes. I shivered. My windbreaker had a warm lining, but a heavier jacket would have been a better choice.

Dolly wiped sweat off her brow, stood up and began the trek up mountain range number three. The mountains all looked alike to me. They all smelled like rotting vegetation, but not in a bad way. They were cluttered with dead tree branches, giant logs, prickly bushes, layers of dead leaves and the despicable villain—poison oak.

I gulped some very fresh air and fell in behind Dolly. As usual, Solow led the way along another deer trail. Was he following a scent, or was he taking himself for a walk? In any case, we hadn't found a single clue. Dolly stretched her little legs upward, one after the other while I forced myself to keep up.

The top of mountain number three was broader and flatter on top than the other two. We walked about half a mile across the ridge, following a deer trail. Finally, the trail headed down toward a deep canyon. We half walked, half rolled down the incline. Near the bottom we saw the remains of a recent mud slide.

"This doesn't look good," Dolly shouted back to me.

"Solow!" I yelled, "Solow come back!"

CHAPTER 22

Solow had the good sense to stop near the bottom of the mountain before he could be sucked up by the deep mud. But he didn't obey my calls to come back. Instead, he hung a right and ran along the edge of the dark goo, nose to the ground.

Suddenly, Solow howled long and hard.

"Dolly, I think he found something," I said, passing her up and running after my dog, suddenly feeling empowered with a spurt of energy.

"Alicia!" I called out.

"I'm right behind you, Josephine," Dolly sputtered.

Solow stopped quick.

I stopped quick.

Dolly ran into me, knocking me flat.

I pulled myself up feeling lucky that I just fell into filthy wet dirt, not deep mud.

Solow howled.

I looked in the direction Solow pointed and saw a small piece of yellow cloth peeking out of a river of solid mud that was easily ten feet deep.

"What's that?" Dolly shouted.

"I think it's Alicia's Ja…" I choked.

231

Dolly grabbed a long stick and began poking at the material. Finally, she was able to tunnel the small end of the branch into the yellow sleeve sticking up in the air. As if she were hauling in a giant sea bass, she sat down, braced herself and pulled with all her might. Everything but the sleeve was coated with mud the consistency of chocolate pudding, making the jacket as heavy as Solow after a big meal.

The bowed branch threatened to break under the weight.

I held my breath.

Finally, the jacket sleeve was close enough to the bank for me to reach. I hauled it up onto a boulder. Obviously it was an empty jacket and we still didn't know what had happened to Alicia. I refused to think of her at the bottom of the mudslide. Instead, I'd have to think of her without a jacket. How many cold winter nights could she survive?

Leaving Alicia's jacket on the rock, we continued our trek.

Solow ran along the edge of the muddy ravine heading north. All along the way there were fallen trees and giant rocks bogged down in the mud. As we marched north, the mud became dark watery goo and eventually morphed into a small stream of actual water. We were thirsty, but the murky water looked unfit for drinking.

"I think we can cross over here," Dolly shouted over the roar of the tumbling brook. A couple feet from shore sat a large flattish boulder, its mossy top above water, and two more large rocks beyond that one. They were enough to get us to the other side.

Solow held back, probably waiting for someone to carry him across the rushing water. There was no way I could balance from rock to rock with almost fifty pounds of basset in my arms, so I called to him and encouraged him to swim.

"He's not coming," Dolly moaned.

"When we start hiking up this mountain, he'll come around." I said, hoping I was right.

A couple minutes later, we looked back, as my soaking wet dog tried to catch up with us. More for our sake than his, we sat down on a log to rest.

The minute he caught up to me, Solow began shaking off river water.

"Oh yuck!" I said, jumping up and trying to get out of range.

Dolly giggled, "Sorry, didn't mean to laugh."

"It's cold on this side of the mountain," I said; "we better get moving."

"You're right, and it's already getting dark," she added, using short quick strides to pull herself up the steep incline.

Solow led us to another deer trail and began following it with gusto—so much gusto that we lost sight of him. I liked to think he did it with Alicia in mind, but who knows what a basset thinks. I had a lot of time to think while climbing endless mountain ranges, but I tried not to think because my thoughts usually involved bad scenarios. Trying to stay positive, I put one damp foot in front of the other and pushed my aching legs forward.

"Dolly, listen…"

"Oh my, sounds like another helicopter. But it's too far away."

"Probably leaving since it's going to be dark soon."

"Dolly shouted back to me, "Josephine, I can't see the trail.""

"I know what you mean," I gasped. "Maybe we should find a place to spend the night." Even as I said it, mental pictures of mountain lions, bobcats, rattle snakes, raccoons, skunks and spiders freaked me out. How could I sleep with all those critters cluttering up the neighborhood?

By the time I caught up to Dolly, she'd already picked a place to spend the night and was clearing away twigs and brush.

"You are...the pioneer... woman!" I exclaimed, sucking up all the air my lungs would hold.

"Maybe that's why I feel so comfortable in my Roaring Camp dresses and bonnets," she chuckled.

I couldn't see Dolly's face, but I knew from her tone that she enjoyed putting her camping skills to work. I was glad she couldn't see my frightened face. Night had fallen on the dark side of the mountain, and all I wanted to do was cry.

"Josephine, take these and start a fire," she said, handing me four stick matches. "I'll save the rest in case we spend another night out here."

"Another night, are you kidding!"

"No. I figure we're somewhere between San Lorenzo Avenue and Toll House Gulch Road."

"What if we're too far north and we miss Toll House altogether?"

"We'll just think positively," Dolly murmured, as she dumped an armful of little sticks and branches on the ground. "Let's hope it's dry enough to burn," she said as she felt the ground for more fuel.

Eventually, we had an itsy bitsy campfire going, with the help of three out of four matches. I gave Dolly the last match for safe-keeping. We warmed our hands over the fire while Solow snored the snore of an overworked basset.

"Josephine, I hate to ask you this, but do you know if Solow's following a scent or just on a hike in the woods?"

"Like you, I've been trying to figure that out. It could be just a basset joy-ride. But he did find the jacket."

"Josephine, this Iggy fellow told you that Alicia ran away Sunday night. That was four nights ago. Where could she have been all this time?" Dolly fretted. Even Ms. Pioneer was wearing down, but turning back was not an option. We needed to see what was over the next mountain. We needed to find Alicia.

"Tomorrow, let's remember to call out Alicia's name more often," I said, silently hoping we'd have the strength to do that.

Dolly didn't answer but I heard her deep breaths. Only a pioneer woman could fall asleep on top of moldy leaves with a few small, leafy branches to cover her. I stripped a couple branches from a young tree and spread them over my shivering body. Silently, I prayed we wouldn't be eaten by wild animals, and we'd find Alicia the next day.

As I slept, I dreamt that Solow and I worked in a museum without walls where people came to watch wildlife and throw coins into a fountain. As I watched people throwing coins, I realized that the bears and raccoons were tossing their coins as well. I tried to stop them from throwing away their money, but they wouldn't listen. When one of the tourists visiting the museum threw a coin, it accidentally hit a bear.

Solow barked at the bear.

The bear turned to lick the woman.

She panicked and screamed over and over. Little distant screams I could hardly hear.

I ignored Solow's distant howls, thinking I was still dreaming.

"Josephine!" Dolly whispered.

I opened my eyes.

"Josephine!"

It wasn't completely dark, but the sun wasn't quite up yet.

"I hear something," Dolly whispered.

"Why are you whispering? We're a million miles from anywhere," I croaked.

"Seriously, I hear something. Solow heard it too. Listen…"

I waited quietly and did hear something. It sounded human. "Could that be Alicia?" I whispered.

"You're right, Josephine; we don't need to whisper, but we do need to take a look."

Already on my feet, I saw Solow posed a few yards away, pointing north, down the hillside we'd already climbed. The eastern sky grew brighter by the minute. He sniffed the air and didn't move until I was just a couple feet from him. Dolly was close behind me. Suddenly, Solow galloped down the slope, disappearing into thick foliage.

"Did you hear that?" I asked Dolly.

She nodded, and we listened, holding our breath.

The sky lightened.

Solow howled and then barked.

We crashed through bushes, not waiting to find a trail, heading straight for Solow's bark. We came to the same little brook we'd crossed the day before, but farther downstream.

Solow howled urgently.

Dolly and I ran through a clearing and charged through more bushes, not paying attention to what type they were. I thought I heard something and stopped to listen.

Dolly plowed into me.

"Did you hear that?" I asked, not even registering pain in my heel.

"No...oh, wait a minute; I heard someone laugh," Dolly said.

We looked at each other for a moment and then burst through more dense undergrowth into an open area. The stream was only twenty feet away, and beside it sat a dirty shivering lump. Solow licked the lump, wagging his tail and letting out a serious howl now and then.

"Allie!" I screamed, as I raced toward her.

Huddled into a ball, she looked up and her whole dirty face smiled.

The sun eased up into the eastern sky as Dolly arrived on the spot—the tiny spot on a map, somewhere within a giant landscape of endless forested mountain ranges.

CHAPTER 23

Alicia, Dolly and I sat quietly in the morning chill waiting for our bodies to warm up before we began looking for a way out of the forest. Our reunion with Alicia had been full of happy tears, but we weren't out of the woods yet.

Fortunately, I had a good sense of direction, especially when we'd just watched the sun rise up from the East.

Dolly seemed to have the most energy.

Alicia sat slumped on the ground against a mossy log wearing my jacket. She had the most scratches and bug bites, not to mention a black and blue stubbed toe after she'd lost her shoes in the muddy creek two days ago. As I suspected, she was not the pioneer woman type. I knew she was strong, hardworking, talented and dedicated to her family. But she never cared for camping or hiking. Alicia was more the "Zoomba" and "Yoga" type. She was so good at yoga, she could have taught the class. Sonia, our yoga instructor, had asked her if she'd like to work as a yoga substitute teacher but she wasn't interested.

We took a few more minutes to soak up the sun's puny rays. It just felt good to be together, to enjoy the fact that we were all alive and mostly well. Alicia told us how she'd fallen in the dark and rolled into the ravine full of mud two days ago. Her jacket was full of heavy mud and she thought it might pull her down. Barely escaping from the mud, she left the jacket behind.

With Dolly and me helping, Alicia stood up slowly. A minute later, she plopped down on a boulder. She talked to us while encased in crusty dry mud from head to toe, looking like a clay statue. To me she seemed ironically out of character, since she was always the most perfectly clean person I'd ever met.

"Allie, some good things have happened while you were gone."

She gave me a hopeful look. "Del?"

I nodded. "Remember I told you that the stranger we named Roger was staying with David because he had amnesia? Well, it was Del; he finally remembered who he was. He joined the search party looking for you. Your brother is a wonderful guy, Allie."

Tears streamed down her face, creating vertical stripes in the dry mud. I wanted to help her wash her face with creek water, but was afraid it would give her a worse chill.

"Allie, I'm curious. What does Del stand for?"

She wiped her eyes. "His name is Antonio Delgado."

"I would've never guessed."

"Jo, how are my boys?"

"Trigger and Ernie are very worried. They'll be so happy when they see you. David, Ben, Robert, Aunt Clara and the whole town have been out searching for you."

"Even Robert?"

I nodded my head. "He shot the boat that Iggy Vargas escaped on."

She almost laughed. "How sweet."

"He said he wanted to sink the boat, so he shot the antenna."

"Bless his heart," she said, "but he obviously needs to practice."

I looked Alicia in the eye, "It was Iggy, wasn't it?"

She nodded. "He didn't hurt me. He said he wanted me to be in good condition when he presented me to his boss, Enrique, Maria's husband. But he did tie my wrists with strips of cloth. I was tied like that for so long I lost feeling in my fingers." She looked at our worried faces. "My fingers are okay now. Oh, if Iggy could see me now," she laughed.

"Iggy Vargas beat up my Howie," Dolly hissed.

"I didn't know that," Alicia gasped. "I'm so sorry that happened."

"The police put Iggy in a line up. Howie and I picked him out, separately. Vargas must have figured it was Howie that fingered him and tracked him down."

"Allie, what was it like...?"

"Sometimes Iggy left me tied up in the back of the van. Who knows what he was up to. Other times, he left me tied up in the shack for hours at a time, but being alone was better than having him around stuffing his face with Cheetos and beer. He sure liked the American diet."

"Well, those little Cheetos bags came in handy," I said.

"So Alicia, how in the world did you get loose from that big old freak?" Dolly asked.

"Yeah, how did you?" I was beyond curious.

"I gnawed my way out. I just kept working at the cloth with my teeth every time Iggy wasn't around. It sounds simpler than it was, but finally I was free. I heard the van coming up the road and I knew

I only had a minute or two, so I hurried out the door into total darkness. I felt my way around to the back of the shack and plunged into the surrounding woods."

"How did you know where you were going?" I asked.

"At first it was all by feel. I had no sense of direction whatsoever. The first stickers and branches I encountered had me all tangled up. Worse than that, I heard the van door slam and a minute later, a lot of cussing in Spanish. I took a breath and just crawled on the ground for the longest time, purposely zig-zagging along. That whole night I imagined he was right behind me. By morning, I realized he'd given up and I was totally lost."

Wide-eyed, Dolly and I finally took a breath.

"Shouldn't we think about how we're going to get home?" Dolly suggested.

Alicia stood up for a moment, teetered and plopped down hard on the rock. "I'm fairly rested," Alicia said, looking at me, "but I need you to do something for me before we try to find our way home."

"Anything!" I said.

"You said you saw my jacket. In my jacket pocket you'll find a little Cheetos bag with my wedding ring in it. I had planned to set it out for someone to find, but the mud took my jacket. I was lucky to get out alive."

"Don't worry, dear," Dolly said, "Josephine can handle it."

I didn't mind at all running a yucky and disgusting errand for Alicia. Even though her ring only had one small diamond, I knew how much it meant to her. I quickly got to my feet—my sore aching feet attached to sore legs and hips. But once I started up the steep trail, things began to move with less pain. Oh, for a hot bath—or a hot anything!

The climb was slow as I dragged my body uphill. Eventually, I noticed that the creek water had turned brown. After ten more minutes of pushing myself to the limit, the brown river had turned into wet mud. Further along, no water was visible, just solid mud. My shoes were caked with it. They felt heavier and heavier with each step. Finally, I sat on the ground and poked my trainers with a stick, loosening clods of partially dry mud. Just as I was about to stand up, I saw a flash of black and white out of the corner of my eye. As I turned my head, the little stinker gave me a blast.

The smell had me throwing up everything in my stomach which turned out to be nothing since I hadn't eaten in a long time. I felt nauseous. The smell was unbearable but I had promised a ring. I pushed myself forward along the bank until I saw a tiny piece of yellow on top of a muddy jacket lying on a boulder. I bent down, grabbed the yellow sleeve and shook the jacket in the air, slinging mud in every direction. Finally I was able to see the outline of a pocket and then another. The first one was empty and so was the second.

I can't go back without the ring!" I cried out to the forest.

I flopped the jacket onto its other side so that the lining was on top. The inner lining just looked like more mud. I felt around, breaking off chunks of crusty goo. Digging around in the furry lining, my fingers came across an opening like the opening of a pocket. I peeled away more dried mud and worked my fingers into the inside coat pocket. It was deep and not clotted like every other part of the jacket.

Pulling out a colorful rolled-up Cheetos bag had me smiling. The ring was inside and came out shiny clean. I took it as a sign that all was well—or would be soon. I slipped the ring on my pinky finger and stuck the bag in my pocket as a souvenir of the infamous trek through a seemingly endless forest.

My return trip back to my friends was quicker and easier because it was mostly downhill. My reception was anything but warm. I wasn't exactly used to my hideous odor, but I'd ignored it as much as possible. My mind was focused on the ring. How wonderful that Alicia hadn't lost it, but my friends had only one thing on their minds.

Dolly put her hand over her nose and mouth and backed away.

Alicia kept blinking and squinting her eyes.

"I'm sorry, you guys, I can't help…"

"Don't worry, Jo, we're just not used to it yet—don't mind us," Alicia gagged.

Dolly looked like she was turning green. "I'll get used to it, Josephine, but we really should try to get home. Why don't you lead…way ahead of us?"

After handing the ring over to Alicia, I called Solow to attention and we began our trek. Any one of us taking the lead was not an option since Dolly and I had to hold Alicia up. Her bare feet were killing her. It was slow going to say the least. Solow knew his business and quickly located a narrow deer trail heading west. With the sun at our backs, we pressed on.

"Since there's nothing coming up soon, just more forest, maybe I should scout ahead," I suggested.

Dolly looked relieved and Alicia smiled. They weren't ready for another mountain. We walked a little farther up the trail until we found a bit of sun and a log to sit on. It would have been a perfect spot for a picnic lunch if we'd had something to eat. But who wanted to eat with the smell of skunk all around us. I was sure I wouldn't be missed as I set about climbing another large hill—small mountain. I knew I was helping my friends to enjoy fresh air by leaving them alone.

Solow quickly found a trail he was enthusiastic about.

I moved along as fast as my mature body and blistered feet could carry me, guessing we were headed west now that the sun was straight up. The trail widened slightly over time, looking like a whole herd of deer had used it. It widened to four feet across at the top of the hill.

I held a hand above my eyes and searched the distant ranges. I was so happy to finally be at the top of the ridge, I almost stepped on a pile of horse manure.

"Oh my God!" I said out loud realizing civilization might be just one hill away. Solow and I hurried as much as we could down the sloping path, a real freeway compared to the trails we were used to.

Something pounded in the distance.

I stopped and asked myself what I just heard. I thought it sounded like hoof beats from an old western movie.

The path turned and there was another pile of fertilizer.

My heart beat fast when I realized steam was coming off the pile. It was fresh!

"Hello! Is anyone out there?" I shouted.

Listening carefully, I heard an animal skitter through the bushes and then a far away, "Hello!"

I walked as fast as I could, stopping periodically to call out. A distant voice echoed mine, and grew louder. Did I hear a whinny? Maybe I was hallucinating due to hunger?

I pressed on.

Heading down the mountainside, the land plateaued temporarily. Thankfully, there were no trees or brushes for a hundred feet or more. Feeling like I was looking at a mirage, I collapsed on a bench positioned at the edge of a large pond. Gazing at the beautiful scene, part of me wanted to wade into the water, but the other part knew it would be very cold. Suddenly, I saw a horse and rider reflected in the water. Was my mind that far gone?

"Josephine...is that you?" a young voice asked. I looked up as Grace rode her horse over to my side. "P U! Where is that skunky smell coming from?"

"Hi, Grace, I'm afraid it's coming from me. How far from anything are we?"

"This pond belongs to Clancy."

I heard myself laugh the laugh of a crazed person.

"You mean we made it to the end of Toll House Gulch Road?" I turned my head to the right a titch and looked up to the flat, bald top of the mountain.

"Who are all those people up there?" They were the size of ants.

She chuckled, "Your friends, silly." Her smile gave me a last burst of energy.

"Grace, here's the situation. Dolly and I found Alicia! Dolly's okay, but Alicia's in pretty bad shape."

"What if we put her on my horse?"

"Yeah, that's what I was thinking."

Grace said she'd been searching the hills all day and would be so happy to help with the last leg of our trip. She said she'd love to call in and report her find, but cell reception wasn't good this far out.

She handed me a power bar.

I started to rip the paper off, but stopped myself.

"Alicia could really use this."

"No problem; I have more in my saddle bag."

I described the area where I'd left Alicia and Dolly. Luckily, Grace knew a much shorter way to get there. She helped me up onto her saddle and led the horse on a winding trail around the mountain straight to the log where the ladies sat. They looked up at the horse as if it were the second coming.

Grace greeted them with her lovely smile and offered Alicia a ride.

I climbed off and Grace and I hoisted Alicia into the saddle.

Poor Alicia, her fuel level was below the red line and maintenance was required. At least on horseback her feet got a rest as she nibbled on a power bar.

Once we were on our way with Solow in the lead, Grace walking the horse and Dolly and I struggling to keep up, we burst into song. About ten rounds of "Amazing Grace" echoed from mountain to mountain as we worked our way toward Clancy's house.

246

David, Ernie, Trigger, Del, Kyle and Rory met us on the last quarter mile of the path. Trigger ran like the wind and was first to see his mother up close. Shocked at Alicia's filthy condition, he paused. Alicia smiled and suddenly all was well in Trigger's world. Grace hoisted the boy up onto the horse behind his mother. His smile could not have been bigger.

The boys gave us mental and physical support, enough to make it up to Clancy's place. Our reception was fit for a queen—or three of them plus one hard working dog. Apparently, the searchers knew we were coming, maybe because Clancy and Howie wore binoculars around their necks. EMT's, fire department, ambulance and police officers were standing ready.

A helicopter arrived from the North, and choppered its way back to Scotts Valley, no longer needed.

Tucked into David's arms riding home, I knew life was good. Who else would come close to me after a run-in with a skunk?

My best friend, Alicia, had been reunited with her husband, her son and her brother.

Dolly's reunion with Rory had been more tender than I would have dreamed. Maybe my opinions of people were inaccurate at times. I'd try to do better in the future.

EPILOGUE

Amazingly, Alicia healed quickly from her wilderness wounds. Her heartache over the loss of her sister, Maria, was lessened by her new access to her older brother. Together, she and Del decided what they'd do with all the jewelry Enrique had lavished on Maria. Del took the pink diamond ring because he had his eye on beach-front property. It was the only piece of jewelry he would accept since his new accounting firm had quickly become very popular in Santa Cruz County.

Eventually, the police returned the two pieces of jewelry to Alicia. She often wore the watch and hair clip in remembrance of her dear departed sister. The rest of the jewels were invested in start-up companies and charities, Trigger's education and a drainage system for Drew Lake. The Quintana's flooded property finally dried up and became a wonderful place to live.

Dolly and Rory drove to Reno and were married in a small chapel with just Howie, Josephine, David and the Quintanas sitting in the pews. The couple had been living together for the last twenty-three years and decided it was time.

Howard was finally called into ranger duty. His first assignment was in Monterey County, prompting him to move into an apartment closer to his work.

Iggy Vargas was never seen or heard from again, thankfully.

Once Josephine was rid of the skunk smell, she and David took up where they had left off.

Just use your imagination!

ABOUT THE AUTHOR

M s. Oroz has turned her "pandemic-time" into "writing and painting time," that is, when she's not tending to her large flower garden. She and her husband and little cattle dog are always busy, even if it's just trimming trees or taking long hikes through their hilly neighborhood. A little gentle yoga at home evens it all out. Joyce loves hearing from her readers at joyceoroz@sbcglobal.net

ALSO BY AUTHOR

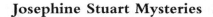

Josephine Stuart Mysteries

Secure the Ranch
Read My Lipstick
Shaking In Her Flip Flops
Beetles in the Boxcar
Cuckoo Clock Caper
Roller Rubout
$cent of a Swindle
Who Murdered Mary Christmas?
Pushing Up Daisy
Hill Street Clues
Dead on a Rifle
Lost & Bound

Non-fiction Books

Muraling for Fun and Profit
Sena's Light

Children's Books

Annie Gets Her Bounce
Annie Gets a Brother
Grady Ghost Has a Secret

Made in the USA
Monee, IL
14 May 2021